THE GOD EXTINCTION

THE GOD EXTINCTION

A DAN KOTLER ARCHAEOLOGICAL THRILLER

J. KEVIN TUMLINSON

KNOVELTON

PROLOGUE

EASTERN DESERT, EGYPT – FIVE YEARS AGO

THE MOONLIGHT WAS A PROBLEM.

Here, on the Western side of the mountain, Amsu was exposed. Anyone in the camp could look up at any time and see him silhouetted against the cliffs. But it was a necessary risk. This was the only path in that was not guarded—a rugged climb over the mountaintop, scaling down a sheer face with only his own hands and feet. A rope would be spotted. It was too risky.

Amsu was a skilled climber, but that was in the daylight. One poor hold, one shift of stone, and he would plummet. But he knew these mountains and cliffs well. He had climbed them all his life, and always without the aid of ropes or special shoes or any other tools. He was amused, when the Westerners worried after him, practically forcing him to take climbing gear. He always left it on the mountainside, once he was out of their reach.

It would only have slowed him down. He would not have

been able to provide for them the information they needed, about the caves and ridges of this region. His usefulness to them would be limited. They would no longer need him, and that meant they would no longer pay him. It had to be this way.

It was his explorations of the area that had led to the discovery of the shaft, his current destination.

Some decades earlier, one of the archeologists from this research site had found something in these hills. Amsu did not fully understand everything the researchers here said about the discovery, but their whispers of it were enough. And he did understand one thing plainly: Within these cliffs was treasure.

That was worth the risk of scaling these cliffs in the late hours, after everyone in the camp was asleep and the full moon was his only light source. It was worth everything, even his life.

The shaft had once been a source of light for some interior chamber. It had been covered by a large quartz stone, about the width of a man's shoulders. During an earthquake, the shaft had widened slightly, and the stone had fallen into its interior. Amsu had found the shaft, had climbed inside, and using one of the small cameras the researchers had given him, he had trans-mitted images back to the camp. They were astonished by what he'd found.

Treasure.

Not gold, but many jewels. Items made of bronze that would fetch a great value, if they were sold. More wealth than Amsu had ever imagined in all his life, and all of it out of his reach, even as he stood inches from it.

Amsu used the camera to show the researchers a sweeping view of the chamber, and they cheered. He could hear them over the little speakers in his ears. It went on for several minutes, as he stood in the treasure vault, listening to them while studying the jewels and statues and walls of this place.

They then told him to come back, and leave everything he'd found.

He went back, but he took one of the jewels with him.

It had once been mounted in a statue of bronze, but the falling quartz had knocked it loose. Amsu had not shown it to the researchers but instead had stooped and quickly slipped it into his pocket, careful to keep the eye of the camera facing the other way. In their celebration, no one noticed.

Once he was back at the camp, he gave the cameras to the researchers and was told to go back to his village. For once, he made no argument or plea.

He waited several days, to make sure no one from the research camp approached him, to ask questions about the missing jewel. They were busy organizing ways to get into the chamber, to use their ropes and equipment, and to have professional climbers do what Amsu had done with his bare hands.

No one knew he had the jewel.

Amsu knew of a man who often came to the village. He was a rich man and drove a very nice car. And he was forever asking about treasure. "Have you seen anything? Do you know of any statues or objects that these researchers have not seen? Can you show me to any places where the archeologists have not yet gone?"

Amsu knew who this man was, and what he was after. He bought treasure so he could sell it to other rich men. And he could make Amsu rich as well.

On one morning Amsu found the man in the village, at the small cafe that the researchers often visited for meals, when they wanted to be away from the camp. The cafe owner counted on that business, Amsu knew, and the researchers were selfish for not eating here more often. That was how Amsu and others felt. The researchers had money and could help many businesses in the village if they would just come more often.

None of the researchers were in the village when Amsu found the man, sitting at a table in the cafe and drinking coffee.

Amsu approached and stood close, silent.

"Yes?" the man asked, perturbed. "I won't give you any money. Go away."

"I have something," Amsu said, quietly. He looked around at the rest of the people in the cafe, but no one was paying attention. Or no one seemed to be paying attention.

"You have something," the man said flatly. "Alright, let's see it."

Amsu took a small piece of cloth out of his pocket and placed it on the table, in front of the man.

The man looked at Amsu's face for a moment, then carefully folded back the cloth, revealing the jewel. He quickly covered it.

"Where did you get this?" he asked.

Amsu knew that it was wise to keep such secrets to himself. Giving anything away meant giving all away.

"It is a secret place. Only I can reach it, for now. But the researchers know of it."

"Is it from their dig site? Did you steal it from them?"

"No!" Amsu responded. "I took it from a cave. I must climb the mountain to reach it. But there are other treasures there."

"How much other treasure?" the man asked.

Amsu knew he had to be careful. He wanted to entice this man, but giving him too much information would be dangerous.

"A few things," Amsu said. "Small things. Bronze. Some jewels."

Again the man studied his face, and Amsu wondered if he might be a mystic. Could he read Amsu's mind? He had heard of such things, and had been warned never to trust a mystic. But this man seemed ordinary, other than his wealth.

"Can you bring me more?"

Amsu considered this. It would be difficult, but he believed he could return to the chamber. It would mean another difficult climb. The moon was different now, as well. Less light. But he knew the cliff face well.

"Yes," he said, finally. "Will you buy this jewel and anything else I bring?"

The man reached into his pocket and pulled out a thick stack of Egyptian pounds. It was more money that Amsu had ever seen in his life.

"Bring me everything you can, and I will pay you for it."

"But the jewel," Amsu said. "You will pay for the jewel now."

It was bold, and Amsu knew that the man could ruin him, if he chose. He could raise the alarm, accuse Amsu of being a thief. The authorities would never take Amsu's word over that of a rich man.

Instead, the man smiled at him and shook his head. He counted out some of the money he'd been holding, folded it, and put it in Amsu's pocket.

"Bring me everything you can," the man said.

Amsu left the cafe and raced away to prepare, though there wasn't much preparation necessary. He grabbed his cloth sack, and a couple of other useful items. And he carefully hid the money he'd been paid, wrapping it in a piece of upholstery cut from the seat of a wrecked automobile, at the village's edge. He buried this deep in the soil, beneath a stone, and prayed over it, that it would be kept safe.

Several hours later, as the night came, Amsu once again scaled the mountainside, in the weak moonlight. He was less worried about anyone seeing him, this time, but more worried about a misstep. He held his nerve, however, and eventually climbed into the shaft.

Once he was a bit deeper in the shaft, he turned on the small flashlight that had been tucked into his pocket—something he'd stolen from one of the researchers. He tilted the light down and held it in his teeth and he made the descent, wedging his knees and elbows against the slanting stone and lowering himself a few inches at a time.

It was slow progress, but once he reached the bottom, he moved rapidly.

He would only be able to carry so much, so he would need to make this raid count. Jewels were the priority, as they were lightweight and small, easy to carry. Perhaps some small statutes or other items as well, but the heavy brass would make it difficult to climb out. He focused on the glimmering stones, illuminated and sparkling in the light of the flashlight.

Using the blade of a knife, he pried at many of the stones, trying to remove them from the brass. They proved much more difficult to remove than he had anticipated, however, and he found he did not have enough strength for most.

It was taking far too much time. Amsu had started his climb at midnight, and it had taken a great deal of time to get to the shaft. The longer he spent here, the closer it got to dawn. He could not risk climbing at a time when the researchers might awaken.

He had almost decided to leave, to be content with the money he now had. As he passed the light around the space one last time, however, it landed on the largest of the stones—a red one, the size of his palm. He peered closer.

This one was set in an amulet of brass, and Amsu had smiled when he discovered it. This would surely bring him enough wealth. The man was sure to be pleased.

He decided that the amulet was enough, and worth the

risk. The rest, he would leave. He would say that this was all he could find. The man would pay him, and it would be done.

Amsu picked up the amulet and played the flashlight over its surface. It gleamed, red and inviting. He smiled and tucked it into the small sack he had slung over his shoulder.

He scanned the room one last time, hoping for more items. He decided he could carry at least one of the small brass statues, carved to look like some squat creature, with its tongue sticking out. It was heavy, but he could manage it. He put it in the sack and cinched it closed.

He had decided this was enough, and was about to make the climb out when he noticed the door.

It was tucked away, behind a bend in the stone cavern, and he'd only caught a glimpse of its outer edge as his flashlight beam passed over the space. It reflected back at him in a golden hue. More brass, he knew, but still it excited him.

He walked toward it. Maybe it was a vault of some kind? It could have other treasures! Coins, jewels, objects easy for him to carry.

The door was indeed brass, and rose high above his head. It was covered in the same strange symbols found everywhere in the cavern. A knotwork of etchings twisted up and around the door's edge. In the center of the door, surrounded by vines of angular symbols, was a face.

It was smooth, and frightening. Like the face of a ghost. Amsu had seen similar faces, carved into stone and wood, recovered from the dig site by the researchers. But this was the first time he'd seen it cast in brass.

He reached out, and put his hand on it, running his fingers over its features.

The face moved under his hand, sinking into the surface of the door, and ...

Its eyes and mouth opened.

Amsu screamed, jerking his hand away and scurrying back into the main chamber. He clambered up and over stones and statues, quickly moving to the shaft. He scrambled up into it and climbed as quickly as he dared, praying for protection as he ascended.

When he reached the surface, the moon had dipped below the distant ridgeline, and the light was scant. He picked his way up the cliff face, reaching for handholds out of memory and hope. He was moving too fast, and he knew it. But his fear was giving his limbs increased strength, and he was keenly aware of every crack and crevice in the stone. Soon he crested the top, and he ran now, making speed down the hillside.

He did not stop until he was back in the village.

The next morning, he found the man, and after some explanations that this was all he could find, he made the sale.

It was indeed a great sum of money. It would get him out of this village. He would start a new life, elsewhere.

But before he could leave, the man grabbed his arm, squeezing hard. "Tell me where you found these?" he asked. "Where is this treasure?"

Afraid, Amsu told him everything he knew. He told him of the climb, and of the vault of treasure, though he had wanted to keep it secret. He described the statues and jewels. "But there is a guardian in the vault," he said, his voice going quiet. "A creature guards it."

"Creature?" the man asked.

Amsu told him about the face in the door.

The man listened, then let Amsu go. "Leave this village," he said. "Never come back."

Amsu was happy to do so. He wanted to be as far from the man and the guardian of the vault as he could be. He never wanted to return here.

He left the man sitting at a table in the cafe, and the man watched him go.

When Amsu had disappeared into the crowd, the man looked again at the amulet and the small statue. He touched the amulet, running his fingers around its engraved edges. He recognized the symbols. He knew what this was.

He cinched the sack closed again, and took out his mobile, dialing a number he had dialed many times.

"I have found it," the man said. "How soon can you get here?"

ROSHARON, TEXAS – PRESENT DAY

Doug's study was a cluttered but serviceable space, with a home-built table festooned with electronics, most of which were scavenged from trash bins and curbsides, and all belonging to previous eras of technology.

Doug was a hobbyist at a different level from most people. He tinkered with the items he found on his morning drives, repairing discarded flat-screen televisions and harvesting components from scrapped computers. It was unbelievable what people would throw away. The previous weekend he'd rescued a Bose Wave radio with a CD player that only needed a lens cleaning to work again. They'd even tossed the remote with it.

Now he placed his newest find—what he referred to as "a box of many things"—on the floor beside his desk. This was something he'd picked up from the curb: A treasure left for him on heavy trash day, when he would make a circuit through local neighborhoods, on the hunt for discarded gems. "Scrap or score," he called it, though his buddy Jimmy preferred the term "junk driving." Either way, it was days like this that Doug lived for. The box of many things was his favorite kind of find.

He opened it and started pulling items out, inspecting them as he lay them on the table. He had a can of Raid at the ready—a first line of defense against a roach invasion. It happened, sometimes.

There was no sign of roaches or any other bugs as he continued to peruse his find, however. Only a growing sense of excitement.

From what he could tell, this was someone's "exit box." The sort of box that gets filled on a person's last day at the office. Maybe they were fired, or maybe they retired. Maybe they died. It was sad, but it happened. And inevitably a box filled with random office supplies and useless junk ended up on the curb, where someone like Doug could find it and mine it for anything valuable.

As expected, the top layer of the box had items that would have been on someone's desk—stapler, daily calendar, a stack of Post-its, that sort of thing. Doug sifted through this and set it aside.

The next layer was where he found the good stuff. Old electronics. A high-end scientific calculator, an old mobile phone, an even older PDA, and half a dozen things Doug had yet to identify. All of this was nested in a tangle of wires and cables, which made the box look intimidating to anyone other than Doug.

On his scale of scrap or score, this was definitely a score! Most of the electronics would be put to use right in Doug's own home office. The rest would be sold or scrapped, depending on what it was worth.

He turned back to the search, sifting through the wires and other debris, and paused.

There was a familiar object at the very bottom of the box,

and it explained why the thing had been so much heavier than it should have been. Buried under the wires and old electronics was a beige, flat, fireproof safe, with a series of numbered dials on its front.

Doug grinned as he moved things aside, making space on his table to place the safe.

The dials on its front were a combination lock. Doug inspected these, trying to spot any wear on them that might provide clues to the combination. None of the dials looked particularly worn, however. No hints, then.

One by one Doug thumbed each dial through an entire rotation, coming back to the digit upon which it had started. Sometimes people were lazy, he knew, and rather than scramble the entire dial they'd move just one digit. After making his way through all six dials, however, the box remained locked.

Next, he tried a series of common combinations. Basic sequences, mostly, such as one through six, both forward and backward, or all zeroes, all ones, all nines. None of these worked.

He sighed then, and turned to his computer. Googling the make and model of the safe, he eventually found a YouTube video that showed the "drill point" for this model. He took the safe to the garage, chucked a bit into his power drill, and got to work.

It took awhile. The metal was tough and thick. Doug had to switch bits at one point, as the one he was using became dulled by the work. But after nearly half an hour he punched through. A puff of white powder emitted from the hole he'd just drilled. He worried, briefly, that it might be asbestos. But he shrugged this off, used a small shop vac to clear it.

He set the vacuum aside and used a flashlight, peering into the newly drilled hole. He could see the mechanism now, and as he once again turned each of the numbered dials, he could spot when the tumblers were set.

Six turns, and a click.

He opened the lid of the safe, his heart beating fast. He tried to keep his expectations low, but when it came to situations like this, where he'd really had to work for it, his hopes were always high.

And he was not disappointed.

Inside the safe, in a foam insert cut to fit precisely, was a round metal object. It had a golden hew to it and looked as if it might have been polished in the past. Now its luster was somewhat dimmed with age, though there was still some shine there.

It looked like a metal jelly donut, if he was being honest.

In the center of the circular piece of metal was a large, red stone. A jewel. The "jelly." And what a jelly!

Doug gingerly lifted the object out of the foam insert, feeling its weight in his palm. On the workbench in his garage, he had a swing arm with a light and magnifying glass, used for close-up work. Doug swung this around and clicked on the light. He inspected the object through the magnifier, turning it over in his hands, leaning in to see every detail.

There were designs etched into the metal. Doug didn't recognize anything, but they did seem somehow familiar. He thought that maybe he'd seen them on the History Channel, or somewhere like that. They encircled the red jewel, on both sides.

Examining the edges, Doug discovered a slotted hole. He turned the object over, looking into the hole through the magnifying glass. There wasn't much to see there, just a couple of slots extending like wings from a rounded hole in the center. He turned the object in his hands, determined to get a better look at the jewel.

As it turned, the light from the magnifier shone through the jewel, casting a red glow into the work table. Doug glanced down, and stopped.

On the table, projected from the jewel, was a strange series of squiggles, as well as three sets of characters similar to those etched into the metal. It looked like writing, though he couldn't be entirely sure.

The squiggles, though ... he knew what those were.

A map.

He adjusted the lamp and held the object—the metal donut, as he thought of it—tilting it and raising and lowering it under the light until the image became clear.

It was as if he were holding a small projector. The image on the table top became distinct and clear. A map, showing the contours of shores and rivers and mountains. He didn't know where this was, but he knew it was a map.

He also knew, for absolute certain, that this was a huge deal.

He was going to be so rich.

CHAPTER ONE

"DESPITE WHAT FILMS and television and thriller novels would have you believe," Kotler said, "archaeology isn't always an adventure."

He was standing onstage, overlooking a large crowd. Behind him, towering over the scene, were three large, red letters: TED. Above that was a large screen displaying a set of artifacts, photos and video of Kotler and other archaeologists at work at a dig site.

At one time he would have assumed his audience was comprised of all college students, with perhaps a smattering of academics and members of the scientific community. Most would have been there to tsk at him, at best, or to debunk him, at worst. That was how many of his public talks had gone, throughout his career.

The events of the past two years had changed all of that.

With many of his exploits still occasionally finding their way into news stories and YouTube videos, Kotler's popularity had grown. He had a fanbase now, it seemed. The people coming to his talks were just as often armchair anthropologists and history enthusiasts as anything, and that was encouraging.

When he'd been invited to speak at TED, he'd considered it a high honor. There was perhaps no more prestigious stage on the planet, and certainly none more recognizable. This was science in the mainstream, and the audience was appreciative, even enthusiastic about the history he'd helped bring to light.

He smiled. "Of course, sometimes it's just as much of an adventure as you might expect from *Indiana Jones* or *National Treasure*."

There was some laughter, which was gratifying, and Kotler continued.

"What's most exciting to archeologists, especially in anthropology and the study of human culture, is usually going to be pretty boring to everyone else. It's a lot of dusting, really." Onscreen was a montage of people hunched over stones, using small brushes to clear away sand and dirt from statues and pottery. "And a lot of stooping over."

More laughter.

"But it's what we're finding as we step back, as we take in the whole picture, that is really intriguing."

The image onscreen changed and morphed, as if a camera were pulling back to reveal a rotating globe. The continents were recognizable, and floating above all of them, like 3D projections emitted from the ground, were glowing images and video of archaeological sites, of artifacts, ancient temples, statues, and other objects. The effect was impressive, as if the entire world were alive with the discovery of history and ancient cultures.

"All around the world, from cultures as disparate and separate from each other as time and terrain can make them, we keep running into something remarkable. From cultures that should have nothing in common, we find commonality."

Several of the images floating above the virtual terrain moved to the center of the screen, aligning with each other. Each image portrayed a repetitive stack of stones—vertical pillars with a large, horizontal stone as a roof.

"You probably recognize the image in the middle: Stonehenge, located in Wiltshire, England. Perhaps the most famous primitive stone structure to survive to modern day, and one that we most commonly associate with early Indo-European culture. These others," Kotler used a laser pointer to indicate the rest of the structures. "Their origins are more diverse, but still part of that Indo-European landscape. Ireland. France. Germany. Spain. This isn't surprising. You'd probably expect those regions to host structures like these."

Now the images enlarged, cycling through a set one at a time as Kotler pointed to each in turn. "But how about India? Jordan? Korea?" He turned back to the audience. "Similar structures, from the same era. And each appearing in cultures that should have known nothing of each other at the time they were built. And it doesn't stop there. Let's go further back."

The presentation advanced, revealing a grid of images portraying hands painted on cave walls. Kotler pointed to each as he spoke. "France. Borneo. Argentina. Australia. North America." He faced the audience. "At a period in history when none of the humans who lived in these regions had the means or technology to travel the globe, they somehow shared commonalities. Not just structures, not just the impulse to make a mark on one's environment. There are symbols—the rudiments of language—that appear across history and cultures, completely disconnected from each other."

Another image replaced the hands, this time of a single symbol that grew to fill the screen. Kotler watched to gauge the reaction of the audience. There was silence, and he knew why. "The swastika," he said. "Perhaps the most recognizable symbol of the Nazis party, and one we have come to associate with hate and horror on an unimaginable scale. But ..."

The swastika onscreen pulled back and fell in line within another grid of images. The audience now saw the symbol represented in a variety of presentations, from simple carvings and sculptures to ornate medallions, from bits of broken clay pottery to gold-laden temple walls. Some appeared in ancient artwork, with motifs ranging from seahorses to eagles. Native American artwork appeared alongside a golden brooch from India.

"The swastika pops up throughout history. Nazi Germany, of course, put it to its most infamous use. It also appears in Russia, no surprise. Also unsurprising, it appears in the US, starting around the 1920s, and not always in anti-Nazi propaganda. But perhaps it would surprise you to see it appear significantly earlier in North American culture, among artwork from early Navajo tribes. These images," he indicated photos of Navajo baskets and blankets, each bearing the Swastika, "predate European settlement of the Americas by hundreds of years. In fact, this symbol is known as the 'whirling logs,' among the Navajo, and it's tied to the story of a great hero. On a journey down what would become known as the San Juan River, in a hollowed out log, the hero encounters a whirlpool, where the San Juan meets the Colorado River. There he meets a Yéi, one of the Navajo pantheon of gods, who teaches him great wisdom. The swastika—or whirling log—is a symbol of great wisdom, given by the gods."

He let that soak in, and noted with pleasure the expressions of awe and astonishment among those in the audience he could actually see.

Kotler began pointing to images on the screen as they

moved by. "Further back, we find the symbol in Iraq, Armenia, Korea, and among what we think of as the primitive cultures. The Anglo Saxons. The Thracians. Even in some neolithic artwork."

He turned and took in the audience. They were quiet, awed by what they were learning. He gave them a break.

The next image was a series of masks, medallions, statues, and paintings, all of which contained figures with one trait in common: Each was sticking out its tongue. To emphasize this, the famous photo of Einstein appeared, his hair wild and his tongue protruding.

There was a beat, and then the audience laughed, breaking the tension.

Kotler chuckled. "We don't really know why the raspberry became a universal symbol among ancient cultures, though we do know that it has a variety of meanings across modern and near-modern civilizations. In Western culture, it's considered a sign of disrespect, while in some Asian cultures it's a sign of chagrin and embarrassment. In Tibet, however, it's actually a sign of great respect. One man's insult is another man's honor." The audience chuckled.

He gestured back to the screen, where several examples of protruding tongues floated above their regions of origin.

"Here we have examples from Ancient Greece, India, France, New Zealand, even the Americas. If we exclude Dr. Einstein..." he paused and was rewarded with a laugh. "You'll note the similarities in all of these figures. Creatures with rounded features, almost like troll dolls, with prominent brows and protruding, pointed tongues. They are typically anthropo-morphized beings—human and animal hybrids. We see the wings of birds, as well as tangles of tentacles. You might recognize the Gorgon, Medusa, her face framed by snakes and, of course, her tongue sticking out. The faces of these creatures are similar enough that they could be transposed from one culture to another and it might prove difficult to tell them apart."

Another grid of images, this time of gods from various pantheons, including an image of Jesus. "Here we see Osiris, Marduk, Adonis, Tammuz, Aliyan Baal, Viracocha, and of course, Jesus Christ. Each of these represents the concept of the 'Dying-and-Rising deity.' That's the shorthand. But there's a more profound mystery here. In every recorded culture, in every pantheon, there exists a god who died and was resurrected. From the Sumerians and Babylonians, the Greek and Romans, the Celtic Druids and even the Mayans and Aztecs, they each have their god of resurrection."

"And there are other commonalities in these pantheons. Gods who not only served the same purpose—a god of harvests, and god of rains, a god of sexuality—but who very often shared histories. Osiris shares a similar origin story with Moses, for example. Both were envied by their siblings. Both had family members who feared for their safety and constructed floating vessels to send them down the Nile. Both are found and raised by Egyptian royalty. The order of these events and the ages of the heroes may differ slightly, but the details are all there."

The audience was wrapt, and Kotler could feel it. Even without being able to read their body language, he could sense what they were thinking, how they were feeling. "In anthropology, we refer to this as 'comparative mythology.' We are looking at these great cultures, at these pantheons and myths, to find the commonality. We want to know why these stories appear, again and again, even in cultures that have never been in contact with each other. And we want to solve the mystery of origin, for the various cultures worldwide. Every ancient culture has a mythology of gods and great heroes. The biggest question we ask, when studying all of these, is where did they go? Were these myths based on actual, living beings? And if so, what happened to the gods, and why did they become extinct?"

On the immense screen, the globe reappeared, rotating slowly, with images and video rising from one horizon and disappearing over the other. The Earth was filling up with the images of archaeological dig sites and ancient artifacts.

"So many cultures. And every day, as we dig deeper into our past, we're discovering more. There is no doubt as to the similarities between each, but the thing that unites them remains a mystery. Where did they come from? How is it possible that they share so many similarities? There are these artifacts, for sure, but there are also shared mythologies. Similarities in oral traditions, in superstitions, in religious observations. Every major culture has a flood myth, for example. There are also myths of powerful prophets, deaths and resurrections, gods walking among men. Over and over, throughout history, we've discovered and rediscovered the hints of a civilization that remains shrouded and hidden. Somehow, in some way, a culture that unites all of humanity came and went, and we barely have any hint of it."

He had their attention. They were wrapt by what he was sharing. The excitement was growing.

"But that's changing. Every day, in disparate parts of the world, we're finding the traces of that extinct civilization. We are writing the history that was lost, with each new discovery."

"Archaeology isn't always exciting. It isn't always about hidden temples or unknown dangers. But the small pieces count. They add up. And the more we learn of this lost world and culture, the more we learn about ourselves. We learn where we've come from, and what it means to actually be human. And that ... that is as exciting as it gets. That's why archaeology and anthropology are so important—just as important as inventing new technologies and exploring new worlds.

By looking deeper into our past, we're learning what it means to be human. And we will carry that knowledge forward, to shape our future. Thank you."

The crowd erupted with applause then, many people standing, cheering and shouting, and Kotler waved to them as he left the stage.

THE TALK HAD GONE BETTER than Kotler had expected. He was glad, but he was also exhausted. The excitement, the tension, the anxiety that came with preparing for this talk was finally asking its toll. As he rode in the hired car, provided by his hosts, he felt himself being lulled toward sleep. He could use a nap.

When they arrived at the bar, however, he exited the car, thanked and tipped his driver, and walked inside. He would have preferred to go straight home, but this was a neutral meeting place. And he wasn't opposed to having a drink— maybe a small celebration for what had been a good day.

Looking around, he spotted Agent Denzel in the back and made his way to the booth where he was seated. Denzel was reading something.

"*The Celts*," Kotler read from the cover. "Roland, I'm impressed! I had no idea you had an interest in ancient cultures."

"Hard to avoid, hanging around with you," Denzel said. He stuck a business card into the book to mark his spot and placed the book on the table. He picked up a glass, about a quarter filled with some amber liquid. "Scotch?" Denzel asked.

"Please," Kotler said, sliding into the booth across from his partner.

Denzel motioned, catching the attention of their waitress, and indicated he wanted two more.

Kotler yawned. "Did you catch any of the presentation?" he asked.

Denzel nodded. "I saw most of it on the live stream, on the flight in. I'm sorry I couldn't be there in person. I just got here about forty minutes ago. I've been in Texas for the past three days."

The waitress arrived with their drinks. "I assume you're off duty," Kotler said, indicating the scotch.

"I am, but I'm still here on business."

"You mean you didn't come to congratulate me?" Kotler grinned.

Denzel shook his head. "It was a speech, Kotler, not a Nobel Prize. Something's come up. And it involves you."

Kotler nodded, taking a lingering sip of his scotch. "Ok, you know me, Roland. I'm always willing to help with a case."

"No, I mean this one actually involves you. Something you were involved with years ago. A dig in Egypt."

"You're going to have to be more specific," Kotler replied, smiling.

"It's about some brass hall you found. And a sword."

Kotler blinked, his drink hovering just in front of his lips. He placed the glass on the table. "The brass hall," he said. "That was ... twenty years ago, I think? Have they found something? Did Dr. Warner reach out?"

Denzel shook his head. "Dr. Warner passed away, about two years ago. His wife passed a few months back. Their kids sold their home and divided up their belongings, but in all that, they threw some stuff out. Some guy found a safe that Warner had held on to, and drilled into it." Denzel turned and opened the leather attache at his side. He fished out an object wrapped in cloth, and placed it on the table, sliding it to Kotler.

Kotler peered at him, wondering, then leaned forward, opening the cloth to examine what was inside.

As the cloth fell away, it revealed a circular and ornate piece of brass, encircling a large, red jewel. Kotler reached for it, but hesitated, looking at Denzel. His partner nodded, and Kotler picked up the amulet, to look closer.

Both sides were engraved with a series of lines and patterns. Kotler recognized them instantly. "Celtic runes," he whispered. He looked up. "No wonder you're boning up. And this isn't in an evidence bag."

Denzel shook his head. "That's because it isn't part of an investigation. I was called in because local law enforcement knew about Historic Crimes. I've spent the past three days helping to run background and clear the guy who found this. He had brought this to the Houston Museum of Natural Science, trying to sell it. They thought he might be an antiquities smuggler, so they called the police. The guy's story checked out, though. The museum is negotiating the best way to compensate him for the find, and I'm leaving that to them. At that point, I was mostly there to determine if there was anything the FBI needed to investigate. Dr. Warner had worked on some government contracts just prior to his death. We were making sure there was no foul play."

"And for that, they needed to call you in from Manhattan?" Kotler asked.

"Well, I think they were angling more for getting you involved," Denzel replied. "Your name is all over the files Warner kept. What files we could retrieve, anyway. The guy who found this said there were all sorts of boxes filled with files and paperwork, but he left all that for the trash collectors. There were a few things in the box that contained the safe. Most of it was written by you."

Kotler shook his head. "I've never seen this object before."

"But you did find that brass hall?"

Kotler nodded. "Oh yes. Evidence of a Celtic presence in ancient Egypt. I found it, with the help of a local guide. And before it caved in on the two of us, I managed to retrieve an artifact—a bronze sword. When we made our way back to the camp, and I showed everyone what we'd found, there was a lot of excitement and interest. And then I was told I was no longer needed for the project."

"Bitter?" Denzel asked.

Kotler laughed. "At first. But no, I got over it. I tried to follow the progress of the dig after that, but I was usually blocked. As an independent, I spent most of my career being blacklisted from one project or another. This one had the potential for a great deal of prestige. Dr. Warner never liked me much, so he had no intention of keeping me on."

"But it was your discovery," Denzel said.

Kotler sipped his scotch and nodded. "It was mine. But then it became his."

Denzel pondered this for a moment, then took something else out of his bag. A sheet of paper. He slid it across to Kotler.

Kotler took it, examining it, and looked up to Denzel. "This is real?"

Denzel nodded. "It's not a will or anything, but it's authentic. Sorry, it took a couple of years to come up. It got buried in that box, after Warner's death."

The paper was a letter, written and signed by Dr. Warner.

TO THE MEMBERS of the council,

Though it pains me to admit it, we must consider including Dr. Dan Kotler in the next phase of discovery, regarding the brass hall and the tomb of Credne. Though funding and local political upheaval have presented near-impenetrable obstacles, *our exploration of the Credne vault produced some of the most profound cultural finds of the century. It is a great burden to me that these finds remain hidden from the public.*

I'll get to the point. I have recently been diagnosed with pancreatic cancer. I am not given much time. I have taken steps to ensure that all of my projects can continue, under competent leadership. This project, however, remains a thorn. The overseer of the site, now under Egyptian authority, refuses to work with this counsel or any other exploratory team, unless that team includes Dr. Kotler.

Dr. Maalyck has made it clear that unless Dr. Kotler is part of future expeditions, the site will remain closed to outsiders.

I have fought this proviso for close to two decades, and now my strength and my time have come to an end.

Therefore, I propose that we invite Dr. Kotler to participate and perhaps even lead the exploratory team. The brass hall awaits, gentlemen, and with it, I believe, the answers we seek. There are treasures of history waiting to be discovered, and secrets of our culture waiting to provide illumination. We are close to uncovering something that will change history as we know it. I would like for my legacy to include its revelation to the world.

Dr. Joseph Warner

KOTLER LOOKED UP, surprised. "Well, this is unexpected."

"It's also a couple of years delayed," Denzel said. "Dr. Warner died before he could submit that letter. The council members he's writing to are part of a diverse University-governed board. A joint operation between multiple programs. Warner was one of the founders, based largely on this find. But none of them ever saw this letter, and the whole thing was shelved."

Kotler sighed. "Of course it was," he said, and chuckled. "I'm shocked that Warner would even think to recommend me, but I'm not surprised in the least that no one else ever considered it." He studied the letter again. "Dr. Maalyck ..." he said. "I knew someone with that name."

Denzel nodded. "Dr. Martook Maalyck. He works with the Museum of Egyptian Antiquities."

Kotler started. "Did you say Martook?" he asked. "It really is him?"

Denzel shook his head. "Really is who?"

"Martook," Kotler grinned. "He was the guide! He and his friends found the brass hall in the first place." Kotler laughed lightly. "Well look what he went and did. He became an archaeologist!"

"A pretty good one, from what I've seen," Denzel replied. "We reached out to him. He's just below the Director, overseeing field work and acquisitions. He was very excited to learn about this medallion thingy."

Kotler laughed. "I don't think that's a medallion," he said. "More like an amulet, maybe."

"Well, whatever it is, Dr. Maalyck was excited about it. Even more excited when he heard your name. He wants to speak with you."

"I'd be happy to!" Kotler replied. "I haven't seen him in twenty years, and then he was just a boy. And not a very good listener," Kotler frowned. "But he had a real sense of adventure. I liked him very much."

"He's flying here," Denzel said. "To retrieve that," he indicated the amulet. "And I figured you'd want to be the one to give it to him."

Kotler smiled. "I'd be honored."

Denzel nodded.

They sipped their drinks, and Kotler said, "So, is that the

business you're here on? You're delivering this to me so I can hand it over to Martook? I mean ... Dr. Maalyck?"

"Well, there's that, and the map."

Kotler frowned. "What map?"

Denzel grinned and picked up the amulet. He took a small flashlight out of his coat pocket and played the beam through the jewel.

Kotler gawked at the table between them.

"That map," Denzel said.

CHAPTER TWO

D<small>R</small>. M<small>ARTOOK</small> M<small>AALYCK</small> was led into the forensics lab by one of Denzel's team. Dr. Ludlum had been gracious enough to let them use one of the examination tables, as well as some of her equipment and tools. She hovered nearby, as curious about all of this as anyone.

Kotler was excited, but he was starting to think that Denzel was even more so.

"This is just kind of neat," Denzel said, a boyish smirk on his lips.

"You've seen secret maps and hidden treasures before," Kotler replied.

"But this time there are no terrorists or bombs or viruses to worry about," Denzel said. "It's kind of nice."

Kotler had to admit, it was a pleasant change of pace. For two years now he'd been abducted and tortured, had dodged bullets, had faced down bombs and nuclear devices and maniacal would-be despots. He had to admit, he missed the simple joys of digging into an ancient mystery without a clock running. It really was nice.

Dr. Maalyck was led into the room, carrying a long, leather case. Kotler barely recognized him. The boy he'd known was now a man in his mid-thirties. He was dressed in a very well-tailored bespoke suit, complete with a bow tie. He wore dark-rimmed glasses that had a vintage look, behind which his eyes glowed with intelligence and interest. Overall he had the appearance of a successful academic—far different from the boy wearing only a pair of ratty shorts and shoes made from car tires. He'd grown into quite a figure.

"Dr. Kotler," Maalyck said, grinning. His voice was quiet, lightly accented, and had a tinge of emotion. He held out a hand, and Kotler took it.

"Martook," Kotler said. "Or should I say, Dr. Maalyck?"

"For you, old friend, I am forever Martook."

Kotler laughed, and the two of them embraced. "I had no idea! You've become quite an accomplished man!"

Kotler had looked into Maalyck's history, after learning he was on his way. After their adventure in the brass hall, and after Kotler's dismissal from the dig site, Maalyck had made a nuisance of himself, appearing daily to help with the work and refusing to leave. Eventually, the researchers grew fond of him, or perhaps decided that he was never going to leave. They gave him tasks, just to keep him busy and out of the way. To their surprise, he excelled at these, and demonstrated an insatiable curiosity for the work.

When Martook was old enough, he entered the University of Cairo, accompanied by multiple letters of recommendation. His time at the dig site had endeared him to many of the researchers, most of whom went on to their own distinguished careers. One of these was Dr. John Graham, whom Kotler and Denzel had worked with briefly. Graham had been the one who found the body of a Broadway star, Maggie Hamilton, in a previously "undiscovered" Mayan tomb. Graham had not been

Kotler's biggest fan, for a number of reasons, and was generally tough on grad students and low-level archeologists. For him to give Martook a letter of recommendation, the boy must have shown extraordinary promise.

Martook—Maalyck— entered the archaeology program at the University of Cairo, specializing in cultural anthropology. From all accounts, he completely immersed himself in his studies, using his past experience at the brass hall dig site to propel himself in his career. Eventually, his zeal for anthropology led to early graduation. His field work was perhaps the best any graduate student had ever participated in, with his choice of sites across the continent and beyond. He'd shown great passion for this work. A worthy career.

Maalyck demurred the praise. "I am honored to do this work. And I have you to thank for it."

"Me?" Kotler replied.

"You showed me the value of knowledge, both practical and theoretical. You introduced me to a world only visible to those who study and work hard to understand. And, of course, you saved my life. I owe you more than I can repay."

Kotler felt a little choked up, but nodded. "Well, you've done very well for yourself, and you're contributing to the exploration of human history. We'll call that payment enough." Kotler smiled. "And now, here we are, with a whole new mystery to solve. Maybe this time you can teach me a few things."

They retreated to the table where the amulet was displayed on a cloth. Hovering above it was a light, and along with the standard magnifying glass, there was also a mounted camera. On a large display behind the table was a crisp, high-definition image of the amulet. The runes and engravings stood out in contrast from brass.

Dr. Ludlum had followed them as they moved into the lab,

and was standing nearby. She and Kotler exchanged light smiles. It had been a few months since the two of them had shared a kiss, after a tense moment near Lake Adirondack. She had saved his life, taking down a trained hitman before he could end Kotler's life.

Since the kiss, they had talked, and had even dated a little. They were taking things very slowly. *Very* slowly. Kotler's luck with relationships, over the past three years, hadn't been stellar. And the fact that he and Liz worked together added some complication. But they'd work it out. He hoped.

"Dr. Maalyck," Kotler said, "this is Dr. Liz Ludlum. She's the Lead Forensic Specialist here in Historic Crimes."

Maalyck took her hand and bowed his head slightly. "It is a pleasure to meet you."

"I've heard a lot about you," Ludlum beamed. "I hope you don't mind if I sit in on this. I've been very curious about the amulet."

"Not at all!" Maalyck said. "But I believe, first, I must correct the record." He turned to the amulet, and lifted the leather case, placing it on the exam table. He opened it, and Kotler felt a shock of recognition.

"That's the sword," he said, looking to Maalyck. "The sword from the brass hall!"

Maalyck smiled and nodded. "It is," he replied, his tone soft, almost reverent. "I have been very fortunate to have had a role in uncovering more of the tomb of Credne. The Ministry of Antiquities honored me by recognizing my role in the discovery of the hall, and this sword. I insisted that your name was added to the discovery as well, Dr. Kotler."

"I received a letter about that," Kotler nodded. "I was honored, but I had no idea you had recommended me. Thank you."

"You were the sole reason anyone knew the hall was there," Maalyck replied.

"So what does the sword have to do with the amulet?" Denzel asked.

Kotler looked up, smiling. His partner rarely showed such interest in these things, and it was endearing to see it.

Maalyck also smiled. "For a start, it is not an amulet, as I have said. It is, in fact, a pommel."

Kotler blinked, and then leaned in for a closer look. "A pommel!" He moved so that he could examine the hilt of the sword, and glanced up to Maalyck. "May I?" He said, gesturing to the sword.

"Of course," Maalyck replied. "This is why I have brought it."

Kotler smiled and gingerly reached into the leather case. He lifted the sword, supporting the blade with his left hand and pinching the hilt between the thumb and forefinger of his right. He raised it so he could look closer at the hilt.

There, at the pommel end of the hilt, was a protrusion of metal. A tiny cross, ornately carved.

Kotler hadn't had much opportunity to study the sword, after rescuing it from the brass hall. His credibility and clout were not yet enough to give him any sway among the academics and other researchers. Soon after his escape from Credne's tomb, he was told that his services would no longer be needed. He had left the site and the project, moving on to other digs and other adventures. It had been two decades since he'd laid eyes on this sword, and he'd forgotten nearly every detail of it.

But this cross had always stuck with him.

He looked up to the others. Denzel and Ludlum were both leaning in, curious.

Kotler smiled, and nodded to the cross, moving it so that the camera could pick up its details and broadcast them to the display.

"You see this, the cross?"

"Hard to miss," Denzel said.

"Wait," Ludlum said, perplexed. "Aren't these artifacts supposed to be Celtic?"

Kotler nodded. "Exactly. So what is a Christian cross doing on the hilt of a Celtic sword, dated to a period almost five hundred years before the birth of Christ?"

He glanced to Maalyck, who was smiling and letting Kotler have his moment.

"I give," Denzel said. "What's it doing there?"

Kotler chuckled. "It's because this isn't a Christian cross at all. It's similar, and there's some speculation that early Christians may have co-opted the symbol, as a means of converting an earlier culture. But it's more likely that this is the symbol of Tanat, more often referred to in Celtic mythology as Dôn, or Dana. She was the Celtic equivalent of the Phoenician goddess of the moon and fertility, Tanit."

Denzel shook his head. "There's a lot to unpack there, Kotler. Are you saying that the Christians stole the cross from the Celts?"

"More likely from the Phoenicians," Kotler replied. "But it wasn't exactly stealing. Maybe 'borrowing' would be a better word. Or ..." he thought for a moment. "*Incorporating*. That fits better. The early Christian church was smart about its approach to conversion. They knew that old beliefs die hard. And so they made an effort to incorporate the ancient beliefs and practices of an existing mythology, symbology, and traditions. Rather than try to fight it, they incorporated all of it into the more modern Christian story."

Denzel looked uncomfortable, and Kotler understood why.

They didn't discuss it much, but Denzel was definitely a believer, and a practicing Christian.

"Think of it as fulfilling the Biblical directive," Kotler said, trying to ease Denzel's discomfort. "That all things serve the Lord. Early Christians knew that symbols and traditions were the keys to making potential converts understand the teachings of Christ. So rather than try to convince converts to give up their old ways, early Christians simply changed their meaning. Whatever traditions or customs a culture had, Christians taught them how those ideas aligned with the teachings of Christ. For example, the Greek symbol, *Ichthys*, sometimes known as the 'Jesus fish,' was previously used in both Paganism and even Buddhism. It came to be associated with Christ through the story of the fishes feeding the multitudes—a clever way to connect ideologies. The vestment robes worn by many Christian leaders were adapted from Pagan practices. And of course, crosses appear in cultures throughout history, most of which predate Christianity by thousands of years. Both the Greeks and the Egyptians used a cross as part of their religious observance, as did the Phoenicians, the Druids, the Vikings."

Kotler saw the expression on Denzel's face and decided to have mercy on his friend. "All things serve the Lord."

Denzel's expression was dubious, and he shook his head. "I grew up with a few folks who would take great offense to all of that," he said.

Kotler nodded. "Probably true. It's not a popular idea. But it's history. People often feel threatened when history challenges their assumptions. They forget that none of this changes the core of their faith. If they believe, a knowledge of history can actually deepen that belief. It has for me. I'm not entirely certain about the truth and reality of a Creator, but the deeper I look into history and science the more I'm convinced that there's something out there. Something beyond my understanding." He glanced around to see Ludlum and Maalyck watching and shook his head, smiling. "At any rate, we're getting off track. The point is, this is not a Christian cross."

He placed the sword on top of the case, at a slight angle, so that the hilt protruded out over the table's surface.

He glanced back to Maalyck. "I think you should have the honors," he said.

Maalyck's eyes widened, and he shook his head, bringing up his palms in protest. "No, I could not. This was your discovery, Dr. Kotler. I brought this so that you could be the one."

Kotler studied him for a moment, then nodded.

He picked up the amulet, feeling the heft of it. He turned it so that he could see the slotted hole. It made sense now. It matched perfectly to the cross on the sword's hilt. Kotler aligned it and then slid the amulet—the pommel—into place. He gave it a turn and was rewarded with a satisfying click as the pommel joined to the sword.

He looked up. Denzel and Ludlum seemed to be holding their breath. Maalyck merely observed, smiling.

"Is that it?" Denzel asked.

"Seems to be," Kotler said.

"Kind of anticlimactic," Denzel replied.

"What were you expecting? It would glow with power? Open a gateway to another reality?"

Denzel scoffed. "No," he said, his tone defensive.

Kotler grinned and picked up the sword, examining it closer. With the pommel now in place, it changed the balance of the sword, giving it a more substantial feel. It felt like it could be used in battle. And judging from the nicks and chips in the blade, it had been. This was not simply art, meant for show. This was a fine weapon, crafted for combat.

And then there was the stone.

"Martook," Kotler said. "In your research, did you happen

to find any information about a map, etched into the jewel of this pommel?"

Maalyck shook his head. "No, nothing about a map. Though we have found hints of the sword being a key."

"A key?" Kotler asked. "To what?"

Maalyck smiled. "That is the other reason I have come," he said. "The sword is to unlock the greatest of treasures—the tomb of Credne, and the gateway to the Otherworld of the *Tuatha dé Danann.*

CHAPTER THREE

THEY WERE USING the large conference room within the FBI's Historic Crimes division. Kotler and Maalyck sat across from each other. Denzel was leaning against the coffee station, having served each of them a steaming cup.

Maalyck slid a set of photographs across to Kotler, and Denzel came around, leaning over Kotler's shoulder.

Kotler arched an eyebrow, and shook his head, smiling to himself. In a way, it was entertaining that Denzel had such a keen interest in all of this. On the other hand, he was being a little lackadaisical about personal space.

"Where are these from?" Kotler asked.

"The excavation site," Maalyck replied. "We have made great progress, though the brass hall itself remains blocked by several tons of stone and debris. In our attempts to dig into it from different angles, we have found several more chambers. Smaller, but there are artifacts within each. One contained pillars inscribed with Celtic runes. Some of the only written records of early Celtic and Druidic tradition."

"Amazing," Kotler said, leaning forward and examining the carvings. "But wait ... some of these are Greek?"

Maalyck smiled and nodded. "It is how we've managed to translate the messages so quickly. While we recognized most of the runes, their groupings made no sense to us until we found their corollary in Greek. There are also Egyptian hieroglyphs and Phoenician writing, all helping to confirm our translations."

Kotler looked up and shook his head. "Unbelievable."

"Why's that unbelievable?" Denzel asked.

Kotler glanced at him. The agent was hovering over him, and in that moment seemed to realize it. He straightened, and then took a seat beside Kotler.

Kotler chuckled. "Well, it's like finding the Rosetta Stone. Multiple languages inscribed in one document—or on one stone. Multiple accounts of the same information. It makes it possible to translate any language we aren't familiar with. The Rosetta Stone was important because it gave us a way to translate languages that were lost to history. This is similar. There are very few written accounts of the Druids, and almost nothing written by them specifically."

"Why's that?" Denzel asked.

"Largely due to the Romans," Maalyck replied. "As the Romans cemented their hold on their empire, the Druids were seen as a threat. The Druids were the intellectual class of the Celts, which made them dangerous to the expanding government of the empire. There was a campaign to destroy anything they produced, which especially included written records. As a result, most of what is known of them today comes from Roman and Greek accounts, and those are highly biased. Accusations of human sacrifice and rituals of dark magic were used to turn public opinion against the Druids, to cast them as figures to be feared."

Denzel nodded. "Propaganda."

"Exactly," Kotler replied, nodding. "And it only got worse over time. But not all was lost. Remember we were talking about Christianity incorporating the traditions and customs of other cultures? That included a lot of Druidic tradition. Early converts among the Druids maintained their practices, replacing prayers to Celtic gods with prayers to saints, to the Virgin, to Christ. It was simple enough, replacing one name with another. The concepts were generally the same. What, really, is the difference between a goddess of wisdom and a patron saint of learning? Rather than surrender and allow their culture to be erased, the Druids instead allowed their traditions to be subverted and absorbed, and then resurrected their practices with Christian themes. And some of those practices still exist to this day, considered to be sacred traditions of the church."

Denzel blew out a breath. "Ok, this is fascinating and all," he looked at Maalyck, "but what did your people learn from all those translations?"

Maalyck turned one of the photographs so that it faced him again. "Most referred to the accomplishments of Credne and his brothers, praising them for their craftsmanship, particularly in forging weapons used in the war against the Fomorians."

Kotler watched Denzel as Maalyck spoke, noting his body language. He saw the blank look. "The Fomorians," Kotler supplied, "were a race of monsters, in Celtic mythology. They were the enemies of the *Tuatha Dé Danann*, the Druidic gods. Where the *Tuatha Dé* represented all that was good and beautiful in the world, the Fomorians represented darkness, chaos, evil."

"Demons," Denzel offered.

Kotler nodded. "For the sake of comparison, yes. In some sense, both the *Tuatha Dé* and the Fomorians could be compared to angels and demons in Christian mythology. Essentially the same race, but their appearance and demeanor and abilities are determined by their natures. There are legends of the two intermarrying and producing offspring. Some of these legends parallel other cultures, such as the Norse gods and the jötnar, or frost giants, in Norse mythology. There are enough parallels, in fact, that some speculate that they share a common root mythology."

"Comparative mythology," Denzel said.

Kotler's eyebrows went up. "Exactly! You *were* paying attention to my talk."

Denzel smirked.

Maalyck placed the photograph back on the table. "In this section, there is mention of the brass hall. Credne's hall. It mentions his tomb as well. But more intriguing was the mention of a gateway to the Otherworld of the *Tuatha Dé Danann*."

"The Otherworld?" Kotler replied. "The home of the gods?"

Maalyck nodded. "According to numerous inscriptions within the chamber, the path to the home of the gods lay with Credne. And to find it, one must 'enter through the mouth of Credne.'" He turned then, and took another photo from a folder in his bag, placing it on the table between them.

Kotler and Denzel both leaned forward at once.

The photo was actually two images side by side, both depicting a face made of brass, mounted on stone. Kotler realized that these were not two different faces, but the same face, depicted with different expressions. "The eyes and the mouth open," Kotler said, glancing up.

Maalyck nodded. "When one presses the face inward, the eyes and mouth open, as does a stone shaft above the doorway. To the best of our knowledge, this is all that takes place. We've attempted to open this door, trying all but destructive force, but it will not budge."

Kotler studied the image closer. "Have you scanned it? Ground-penetrating radar? Ultrasonics?"

"The stone is too thick and dense," Maalyck said, shaking his head. "And we must be careful with some of our scanning methods. We cannot use any method that might trigger activity in the stone. As you are aware, the area is unstable." He smiled at Kotler.

Kotler blinked, then laughed. Twenty years earlier, he and Martook Maalyck had barely escaped the brass hall with their lives. After discovering the hall, and briefly exploring it, they had inadvertently triggered something that caused the unstable stone around them to shift. The caves and tunnels through which they had entered and escaped had collapsed under tons of debris, shutting the hall away under the rubble.

Kotler and Martook had escaped with only their lives and a single artifact—the bronze sword of Credne.

Kotler was looking at the photos, considering. "That opening, Credne's mouth, doesn't look big enough for a person to enter."

"It is not," Maalyck agreed. "We are not certain what the inscriptions are actually referring to. Some wonder if we have misinterpreted them. We have examined the opening, and have found nothing inside but the surface of the stone door. We believe the sword is the key to opening the tomb of Credne. Or the gateway to the Otherworld. Or perhaps both, we really can't be certain. But we do not know how it would do so, or how the mouth of Credne is connected." He took a document out of his bag and pointed to a highlighted section. "Here, you can read the translation."

Kotler took the document.

. . .

T HE OTHERWORLD AWAITS *those who enter through the mouth of Credne.*

T HAT SEEMED CRYPTIC ENOUGH. It presented as a riddle of sorts, but without more context Kotler couldn't yet determine what it meant.

There were other mentions of the gateway, of the *Tuatha Dé Danann,* of the exploits and accomplishments of various Irish gods. But one notable passage caught Kotler's attention:

W HEN CREDNE'S *blade pierces the veil, the Otherworld will welcome the worthy. The path to the gods will be revealed by the eye of Credne.*

"T HIS PART," Kotler said. "Do you know what it means?"

Maalyck examined the passage, and shook his head. "No. The eyes of the visage are made of the same solid brass. Only the lids open. We have located nothing that might be considered a veil, in any of our excavations. We believe this must refer to something either in the brass hall or in some as yet undiscovered chamber."

Kotler was studying the photograph of the face. "This visage, we believe this is Credne?"

Maalyck nodded. "There are several indications within the chamber."

"I know that look," Denzel said. "You figured something out."

Kotler shook his head. "Not so much figured out as come to a suspicion."

He looked at Maalyck. "The mouth of Credne has to be a

reference to this visage. The opening mouth can't be a coincidence, given this passage. But the translation about the eye is singular. That might indicate some other object, and not the visage. Martook, you said that you found references to the sword being a key?"

Maalyck nodded. "It is obscure, but there is a mention of this in the translations. And one of the runes etched into the blade does translate roughly as 'key.'"

"And I think we've found the keyhole," Kotler said, pointing to Credne's open mouth. "Pierce the veil. The word itself, veil, has cultural connotations that go back thousands of years. I think, in this case, it's the veil of death." He looked up. "We don't really know how Credne died. There's no mention of it in Irish mythology. Nothing that has survived to this day, at any rate. But I've been curious about something, since finding the brass hall years ago. I've thought about it from time to time, and now it's really bugging me."

"What's that?" Denzel asked.

"Why Credne?"

Denzel shook his head. "What do you mean? Why not Credne? He's supposed to be a god, right?"

Kotler nodded, then said, "He is. But his part in Irish mythology wasn't exactly a solo role. He wasn't a sung hero, per se. He was always mentioned alongside his brothers, Goibniu and Luchtaine. They were known as the *Sri Dée Dána*. The three gods of art, in Celtic mythology. They were the children of Brigid and Tuireann, two of the most powerful gods in the Celtic pantheon. Basically, Credne was the almost-famous god. A goldsmith who crafted objects that were imbued with mystical properties. Forging weapons for the war with the Formions was about as close to combat as Credne ever got, according to mythology. So when it's all said and done, Credne isn't the sort of god you'd expect to have this level of reverence. So ... why Credne?"

Denzel huffed, and sat back.

Maalyck was leaning forward, his hands together, his fingers resting just beneath his nose.

"I believe it's because of how he died," Kotler said, after a pause.

"But you said we don't know how he died," Denzel said.

Kotler shook his head. "Officially we don't. But I think we've just discovered it." He tapped the photo of Credne, his mouth open. "I believe the sword is meant to enter the mouth of Credne and act as a key."

Maalyck shook his head. "As I have told you, the opening leads only to the stone surface of the door. At best the sword would enter only a few centimeters before being stopped by the stone."

Kotler nodded. "True. Except we know about an old trick the builders used, don't we? When you and I were trying to find our way into the brass hall, we discovered that what appeared to be solid oak from floor to ceiling actually had soft spots. Hidden behind a realistic facade was the trigger for opening the door. All we had to do was cut away the thinner wood with an awl, do you remember?"

Maalyck smiled and nodded. "I do. It was, at the time, the most clever thing I had ever seen."

Kotler laughed. "Well, I think we have another case of misdirection here. It's the language of this translation. 'Pierce the veil.' If the sword is the key, and we're to enter through the mouth of Credne, then it seems reasonable that we have both a key and a keyhole."

Maalyck leaned back, surprised. "That never occurred to me! Nor to my colleagues!"

"I could be wrong," Kotler said, shaking his head. "But it fits. Fortunately it will be very easy to test this theory. All we have to do is put the blade of this sword into Credne's mouth, and push."

Maalyck was smiling. "Then it will be exciting when you test your theory."

Kotler laughed. "Well, I'd love nothing more than to be a part of this, but from what I hear the Egyptian government has most of these sites locked down at the moment. It would take months, maybe years to be cleared."

"Years," Maalyck said, nodding. "It took years."

Kotler shook his head, perplexed. "What do you mean?"

"On my recommendation," Maalyck said, "you were placed on the approvals list nearly three years ago. As the discoverer of the brass hall, and with your long history of contributions to the archaeological community, you are a recognized authority, according to the Egyptian government. If Dr. Warren had not died before sending his letter, you would have been notified by the council that it was considering you for a position with the research team for this site."

Maalyck smiled as he took a letter out of his bag, handing it to Kotler.

It was a letter of invitation from the Museum of Egyptian Antiquities, officially endorsed by the Egyptian government.

"I'm here to offer you the position. We would like you to lead the new team, in uncovering and exploring the tomb of Credne."

CHAPTER FOUR

BEING HERE WAS DANGEROUS.

For years now, the Egyptian government had enforced a lockdown on this and many other dig sites, restricting access with military-level security. The orders were "shoot to kill." No warning shots were given.

Ammon knew the risks, but failure brought dangers of its own. He needed access to this site. And he had certain advantages.

He had plenty of money for bribes, which would help. But this did not give him free access. He would need to proceed carefully, to avoid doing anything that would call the sort of attention to himself that would force the government's hand. They could turn their heads when it came to bribery and trespassing, but only if they maintained plausible deniability.

At this stage, Ammon had to play by the rules, as did his partners. Which meant that he could not rely entirely on his contacts here to protect him if things went awry. Not all of these men were part of the order. Not yet.

Ammon crept among the stones and debris. He clung close

to the mountainside, letting the deep shadows do the work of keeping him hidden. He was making a survey run around the site, probing to see if his intel was correct. It had been several years since Ammon had last been here. It had been nearly two years since his source had seen the site as well, and memories were often untrustworthy. So far, however, Ammon was finding all of the landmarks his source had indicated. The entrance was close by.

Since 2011, and the Egyptian revolution, the government had tightened its control over specific historical sites, in certain regions, preventing access by robust vetting and security. This was spurred, in part, by the destruction of the Egyptian Museum of Antiquities, in Cairo. During the revolution, the museum was raided, and many artifacts were damaged or stolen. Among these, two of the ancient mummies were destroyed. It was one of the darkest moments in the modern era of archaeology, and nearly a decade later the impact was still being felt.

In some ways, it opened the door for the order to further its plans. But the heavy security and restriction of movement and exploration had also slowed progress.

Ammon moved stealthily, eventually finding the path his source had indicated. An iron gate spanned the gap that had been carved into the rock face. Ammon had been told to expect this.

It was a formidable blockade, notably as it included an armed guard—one of the Egyptian military, assigned to prevent anyone from entering.

Ammon whistled, signaling his approach, and stepped into the circle of the security light. The guard dutifully raised his weapon and told him to halt. He didn't shout, but his voice was firm, his intention unmistakable.

Ammon raised his hands over his head and ensured that his face was visible in the light.

The guard looked from side to side, and then lowered his weapon, gesturing for Ammon to join him at the small, wooden shed next to the gate. A guardhouse, of sorts, though it contained only a few odds and ends, primarily a clipboard and some office supplies. There was not even a stool to sit upon.

Ammon stepped into the shadows beside guardhouse.

"*Ahlan wa sahlan,*" Ammon said.

"*Ahlan bik,*" the guard replied. He continued, in Egyptian, "You have brought me what you promised?"

Ammon nodded and took an envelope out of his pocket.

The guard opened it, counting, then shook his head as he put it inside his coat. "Wait here."

He stepped away, into the darkness, and Ammon waited.

He was not nervous, but he was cautious. He knew what was coming, and had planned for it.

Two men accompanied the guard back to his post. They had their weapons raised and demanded that Ammon put his hands up and face them.

"My friends," Ammon said, obeying their orders. "I have not forgotten you. I have brought gifts for you as well."

This was the standard shakedown. The bribes would need to be extended to the guard's compatriots. It was customary. And one of these men was the guard's commanding officer. His bribe must be bigger than that of the other two, which was also customary.

Ammon gestured, silently asking permission to lower his hands. He reached into the inner pocket of his coat, and carefully removed two more envelopes from his pocket, offering them to the two men.

They inspected their envelopes, and without a word, all

three men turned and left. The original guard paused only long enough to unlock the gate and leave it standing open.

Ammon would have one hour. No more. He must make his entrance, do his work, and leave this place before that time counted down, or risk being locked inside. This would inevitably end in his death, as he'd be "discovered" by the guards at some point, who would be obliged to shoot him for trespassing.

Ammon intended to be long gone by that time.

This ingress had been created by the original exploratory team, two decades earlier. They had used small, shaped explosive charges to carve a path into the mountain, to reach the site where the brass hall had been discovered. It was slow and dangerous work and had taken much of the twenty years since the tomb's discovery. And perhaps all for nothing, as the researchers had soon after found themselves stymied by the unstable geology of this region. The brass hall itself remained locked behind a wall of fallen stone, half the mountainside acting as a barrier to entry.

They had found other sites in their progress, however. These mountains were apparently honeycombed with vaults and rooms, many of which contained ancient Celtic artifacts. Some also held Egyptian treasures—making them entirely subject to Egyptian governance.

Ammon needed access to one particular vault.

He would have preferred to enter via the shaft, through which the vault had initially been discovered. But this had been blocked and sealed for nearly five years, as the research team had managed to cut an access to the vault from below. There had been suspicion of thieves gaining access via the shaft, and so it had been sealed, along with any path to it. This was the only way in now.

Ammon carefully picked his way up the stone slope, and

once he reached the opening to the vault, he crept inside, stooping to crawl through the low-ceilinged entrance. He turned on his small flashlight, illuminating the sloped stone of the entrance.

He emerged inside the vault, surrounded by artifacts of stone and brass, all cataloged and labeled by the researchers. It was an odd sight, as if someone had built a museum exhibit in a cave in the middle of nowhere.

This was the safest location for all of it, these days. Protected by miles of stone and the might of the Egyptian military, only those brave enough—or insane enough—could gain access, and at significant risk and expense. Most thieves felt it was not worth the time and effort. Anything stolen from this vault would be difficult to sell.

Ammon was no thief, however. He had an objective. And it would be worth the risk.

Standing within the vault, he oriented himself according to his mental map, a combination of his previous experience here and of what records he could uncover about the layout of this place. It all had to be carried in his head. He could not risk carrying a real map, or anything that would indicate what he was after. He had risked enough by sneaking the blade in.

He took this out now, withdrawing it from a custom scabbard sewn to the side of his coat, and stood facing the door. Before him, the face—a brass visage of the Druidic god, Credne—had its eyes and mouth closed. Ammon placed his hand on the face and pushed.

As it sank back into the door, its eyes and mouth opened. An eerie and frightening sight, but Ammon had known it would happen. It was necessary. It revealed the lock.

He held up the blade.

It was a replica of the sword recovered from the brass hall, two decades earlier. It was made to exacting specifications, even including the nicks and chips in the blade. It had no hilt, however. This would have added bulk and made the blade more challenging to conceal.

Ammon held the blade, resting it on his palm and aligning it with the opening of Credne's mouth. He then inserted the blade into the mouth, feeling some small resistance at first but continuing to push until it would go no further. He could feel the mechanisms engage as he pushed, a symphony of satisfying clicks and gentle resistance.

There was the sound of stone moving against stone, and Ammon stepped aside, taking shelter under a nearby archway, in case the ceiling caved in.

He waited.

Nothing happened.

Stepping closer to the door, Ammon pushed, but it did not budge. No matter how hard he tried, the door remained firmly closed.

He stood back from it, examining it closer, frustrated to have come so far only to be denied entry.

Had he been wrong? Had this been a mistake? He had invested so much into this, had risked so much. Was it for nothing?

That was when he noticed the moonlight.

It had been pitch black in the vault when he entered. He lit the space with his flashlight, which sat off to the side now, casting its beam on the wall next to the door, the spill of its light creating a dim reflection on Credne's brass face. Ammon had reached out to touch that face, wondering about his mistake, and noticed a faint, blue cast on his arm.

He turned off the flashlight, and let his eyes adjust.

There. Ammon saw it clearly now. Motes of dust floated and danced in a beam of moonlight, emitted from the ceiling, casting a tight circle on the floor.

He looked up and saw that a new shaft had appeared above him. A stone in the ceiling had moved, opening a crack wide enough for moonlight to enter the chamber. It was faint but visible. In the daylight, it would be a bright beam in the relative darkness of the vault.

Ammon looked at the floor, where the beam of light struck. There, carved into the stone, was a pattern. It twisted and curved, rose and fell. It was little different from the design that spanned the rest of the floor of this space, but with the moonlight striking it Ammon could see that it was, in fact, distinct.

He took out his mobile phone, and took several photos, sending them to a folder in cloud storage. He then deleted the images, in case he was captured, and his phone was confiscated. He would examine these later.

For now, he had to admit at least partial defeat. The blade of the sword had indeed worked as a key, just as he'd suspected. But it hadn't opened the door. It had only managed to reveal a new riddle.

Ammon removed the blade, and with the sound of stone grinding the beam of moonlight disappeared. He used the light of his phone to retrieve the flashlight and turn it back on. He tucked the sword blade back into its hiding place within the folds of his coat and left the vault.

The gate still stood open, and no guards were in sight. Ammon exited and hurried away, once again clinging to the darkness and the deep shadow of the mountain. He moved as silently and cautiously as possible, hiding among the stones if there was any sign that someone might be near. His bribes had given him only enough safe passage to enter and exit the vault. The guards would not hesitate to shoot him, now that their contract had ended.

Nearly two hours later he arrived in his room, at a small, abandoned inn he had purchased on the far outskirts of the village. He locked his door and sat at the table he used as a desk. He cleared some of the reference books and other items, and placed the sword before him, under the light. He debated what he should do.

He had counted on gaining access through that doorway. He had been right, about the door and the sword. This excursion had cost him dearly, but it had confirmed what he knew. The order would at least be pleased to hear that. He hoped.

It was not enough. The gateway to the Otherworld of the *Tuatha dé Danann* remained closed to him and to the order. Now, however, he believed he knew what was missing.

He needed the real sword of Credne. And that was in the possession of the Museum. Specifically, it was in the possession of Dr. Martook Maalyck.

Ammon's old rival. The favorite. The prodigy who had caused Ammon to be banished from the site before completing his work.

Ammon began making new plans. He would need to explain his failure to the order. He would need to request more money, for more bribes. He would make a second attempt. And this time, he would be truly armed.

He would have a sword.

CHAPTER FIVE

John F. Kennedy International Airport

KOTLER STILL FELT bemused by it all, even as he took a seat in the airport lounge. His flight would leave in just over an hour, and he meant to make use of the time to finish up a few last-minute tasks. He'd made preparations, canceled some overlapping engagements, and arranged for people to cover for him in various functions. The most difficult was his hiatus from his consulting work with Historic Crimes.

He'd taken breaks from case work with the FBI in the past, but this was different. This time he wasn't running, wasn't trying to escape some problematic emotional event or recover from being abducted or tortured. This time, he allowed himself to admit, there was the distinct possibility that he was leaving Historic Crimes for good.

He hadn't yet decided.

For two years he had helped Agent Roland Denzel and the FBI to solve crimes related to history. It had been a roller-coaster, for sure. In that time he'd been shot, tortured, and manipulated. He'd been endlessly chased by armed mercenaries, and had barely escaped with his life on a number of occasions. For two years he'd somehow, through wit and luck, managed to survive.

In that time he had also formed a friendship with one of the most remarkable men he'd ever met. Agent Roland Denzel had become a vital part of Kotler's life, and his dearest friend. Though he knew Roland would be wildly uncomfortable discussing it.

Kotler had also become a vital part of an organization that was doing good work in the world. Historic Crimes, though inappropriately named, was a unique and inspiring concept in law enforcement. Kotler had to admit, he liked being able to apply his expertise and knowledge to puzzles brought to him by the FBI. There had been personal costs, however. Because of this work, Kotler had suffered losses that still ached within him.

Still, the work was fascinating, and through it Kotler felt he was doing something truly good in the world. Danger would always be part of it, but that wasn't necessarily a reason to walk away.

And, of course, through this work he'd met Liz Ludlum.

If he were being honest, Roland and Liz were the two people who gave him the most pause, when considering a transition. Leaving his consulting position with the FBI wouldn't necessarily end these relationships, but it would make them more challenging to maintain. Burying his head in the sand and stone of Egypt, exploring an enigmatic and out-of-place archaeological enigma, would become a full-time occupation.

It would change things.

But that's what this hiatus was all about. He would figure it out. Things would work out fine, one way or another. This trip was about discovering which path was next for him, whether he wanted to step into this role, to make this change in his life and career, or to stay on the path he'd traveled for the past two years. It was about exploring who he really wanted to be.

It would work out fine.

He had just opened an email to a New York colleague when someone dropped a heavy duffel bag on the floor beside him.

Kotler looked up, startled.

"Roland?"

"Surprise," Denzel said flatly. Then smiled.

"What are you doing here?" Kotler asked.

"Well, first off, it wasn't easy figuring out where you were. I should have known you'd be in a fancy airport lounge instead of out in the terminal with the commoners."

"I have a membership," Kotler blinked, a bit dumbfounded.

"I don't, but luckily they take credit cards."

"Roland ..."

"I'm going with you," Denzel said, smirking. He dropped into the chair across from Kotler. "I took some vacation, and I'm going to Egypt. Got it cleared with their government and the museum and everything."

Kotler shook his head. "I'm ... what?"

"Unless you don't want me there?" Denzel asked.

Kotler shook his head grinned. "Oh, I think having you on a dig would be just about the most amusing thing I can think of. But I'm just ... surprised."

Denzel shook his head. "I just think it's interesting. And I wanted to see it for myself, after everything Dr. Maalyck showed us. I had some PTO stacked up, and the Director has been giving me a hard time about it. So, this seemed like as good a chance to get away as any."

Kotler studied his friend for a moment. There was something in his body language that didn't quite line up. "Roland ... are you here to make sure I come back?"

Denzel didn't answer immediately but instead picked up a drink menu. "I'm on vacation," he said, his head tilted down, his features obscured.

Kotler smiled and laughed lightly. He leaned back and sighed. "Well, if you're going to be on this site, you'll have to pull your weight. Remember, I'm the one in charge on this one."

Denzel nodded. "Of course," he said. "Whatever you need."

"Crawling into caves under the desert ... that's mostly what I'll need."

Denzel's face went a bit pale. Kotler was pushing his buttons. He knew that his friend suffered from claustrophobia, with origins in a collapsed spider cave in Afghanistan. It was a nagging problem for the agent, though he'd shown remarkable progress in overcoming it. Still, Kotler knew the thought of tight spaces, particularly underground, would be difficult for Denzel. In a sense, this was a gentle warning.

After watching Denzel's mild discomfort for a moment, Kotler gave his friend a break, smiling. "Maybe I can find something for you to do at camp," he said.

Denzel seemed relieved, nodding slightly though he made no sound.

Kotler turned back to the email he'd been writing, finishing it up. Soon it was time for their flight, and he and Denzel grabbed their bags and made their way to the terminal.

They talked casually. Denzel seemed lighter somehow, but also seemed guarded. Wary.

He's worried I'll leave permanently, Kotler thought as they got to the business of boarding their flight. They split at the gate, with Kotler taking a first-class seat and Denzel, ever the pragmatist, working his way to coach.

As Kotler settled in, a drink at hand and a book on his iPad, he was taken with one thought.

He may have good reason.

Credne Dig Site, Egypt

The dig site was more than eight hours from the Cairo International Airport, through mountainous and rough terrain along the Gulf of Suez—a long and grueling ride that did not always stick to established roads.

They first disembarked at the same village where Kotler had spent many off-hours, twenty years earlier. It wasn't exactly a hot spot of tourism, but it had an active marketplace and a few amenities. The cafe in which they sat was dingy and open-aired, but there were several other patrons. The meals here were simple fare, and the strongest beverages were teas and coffees. But it was a pleasant spot, with lively conversation all around, lulling Kotler and Denzel into drowsiness after their travels.

They would be picked up by a local driver soon and taken to the camp. For now, it was simply nice to not be jostled in an overcrowded bus.

The village—which to this day appeared to have no name—hadn't changed much in twenty years. Signs of extreme poverty were still everywhere, though the marketplace teemed with activity. Vendors sold mostly fruits and vegetables from small, covered carts, but among them were displays of other goods. Locally sourced pottery, baskets, and jewelry could be bought here, though Kotler knew that the locals themselves had little use for or interest in most of these items. They were meant almost exclusively for the foreigners who came here on various business. There were the researchers, who had thinned out somewhat since the "Days of Rage"—the Egyptian revolution in 2011. More prominent was the oil interest crowd, who were the most appreciated among the villagers, as they freely spread money around.

Of course, there were also those with more illicit interests. The market for stolen antiquities, particularly treasure, was still alive and well. Human trafficking had also become a problem in the region, as had narcotics, which were primarily supplied to the visiting foreigners. Of all these, however, the local authorities were more concerned with alcohol, which was restricted here. Foreign visitors often paid top dollar for a bottle of cheap bourbon, and so there was quite a black market.

Perhaps as a redeeming feature, this region seemed particularly rich in archaeological finds. Since the late nineties, thirteen separate sites had been opened and explored, with discoveries ranging from shards of pottery to lost tombs. Most interesting to Kotler, as he had brought himself up to speed on the state of the region, was that the brass hall was not the only cultural anomaly uncovered here. This area seemed to be a melting pot of sorts, if the hints revealed by researchers were an indication. It was unfortunate that exploration here had all but stopped, thanks to the same government corruption and public strife that had led to the uprising.

Research and exploration had resumed at numerous prominent sites across the region, but some, in more remote areas, had been stymied for years. Perhaps the reopening of this site, and the invitation for Kotler to lead the team, were good signs.

Kotler and Denzel sat at one of the cafe tables and sipped coffee strong enough to peel paint from a battleship, but enjoyable for its steamy richness. They nibbled on a plate of olives and dates, and scooped hummus with bits of pita bread. They were both dazed and exhausted from two days of hard travel, and each wanted nothing more than to finally reach their destination and collapse onto a cot for a few hours of sleep.

"Dr. Kotler?"

Kotler looked up to see a man dressed in linen, with a scarf wound loosely around his neck and pulled like a hood over his head. He smiled and extended his hand. "I am Dr. Nesahor. I have been sent from the camp, to retrieve you. It is a great honor to meet the man who discovered Credne's tomb!"

Kotler took Nesahor's hand and returned the smile. "I'm pleased to meet you, Dr. Nesahor. But I can't take much credit for the discovery. Dr. Maalyck deserves it more than I do. He led me to the chamber when he was still a young boy."

Nesahor nodded. "We have all heard the stories of your adventure. You had the presence of thought to retrieve the bronze sword before the collapse of the mountain. That artifact has been instrumental to the continued preservation of this camp."

Kotler nodded, pleased that he was remembered but unsure if he deserved so much credit. Clearly, Maalyck was telling these stories, coloring them with admiration.

He turned and motioned to Denzel.

"This is Agent Roland Denzel, of the FBI."

"The FBI?" Nesahor said, astonished. He offered his hand.

"I'm here unofficially," Denzel replied, shaking Nesahor's hand. "I had some time off, and I'm interested in what you're doing here."

Nesahor nodded. "We are honored to have you with us." He looked to Kotler. "I have a jeep parked nearby, and we can be at the camp in less than an hour. If you will come this way?"

Kotler and Denzel rose, following Nesahor through the streets of the village. At one point they were suddenly swarmed by a flock of children, shabbily dressed and gesturing to them wildly, begging.

Kotler smiled and doled out coins and candy, a stash he'd made sure to have on hand.

"Mind your wallet," Denzel grumbled to him. Despite his apparent wariness, however, Kotler noted when Denzel slipped his own little treasures to the children while struggling to keep a smile from his lips.

"I forget, you've had at least as much experience in this region as I have," Kotler said as they finally arrived at the Jeep.

"Probably not quite as much, but plenty," Denzel said.

Kotler nodded. Denzel's time in Special Forces had included tours of this region, as well as Afghanistan, two-thousand miles to the East. Kotler had never pressed Denzel for details about his exploits while in the service, but he knew Denzel had gotten around. Maybe one day they'd have a chance to sit and chat, to trade war stories, as it were.

They reached the Jeep and climbed in as Nesahor started it up and pulled slowly away, allowing the flock of children to part around them like a ship passing through ocean waves. As the path opened up, they picked up speed.

The village was only a short distance from the campsite, as the crow flies, and perhaps would have been quicker to reach on foot. The rough terrain could be challenging, however, and as tired as they were it was a blessing to have ground transport, despite adding most of an hour to the journey. They were in no hurry. Denzel dozed while Kotler, trying to be polite despite his weariness, chatted amicably with Nesahor.

It was useful conversation, and Nesahor filled him in on the current state of the camp, on the presence of Egyptian military, and on the political climate of the area. If Kotler took on the role of leading this expedition, he'd have to manage all of these elements, on top of keeping the research and exploration going.

Still, he could have used the nap.

The road wound through the mountains, snaking its way through a pass cut into the hills. In essence they were looping around one of the larger mountains in the area, until they were once again just south of the village where they'd started, only three or four miles away from the dig site. Eventually, they arrived, and Kotler and Denzel said goodbye to Dr. Nesahor for the moment.

They were led first to a large tent. "This will be Dr. Kotler's quarters," their guide replied. He looked to Denzel. "Yours are further on within the camp. I will guide you."

Denzel nodded, and looked to Kotler. "Shuteye?"

"The most shut of eyes," Kotler agreed, nodding and yawning. "I've set up a camp-wide meeting for the morning. You'll be there?"

"You're the boss," Denzel shrugged. "You tell me where to be, I'll be there."

"Be there, then," Kotler smiled, and they parted.

Kotler entered the tent, which was quite a bit larger than what he was used to, and with far more amenities. Leadership had its privileges.

It was, in some sense, a house made of cloth, complete with room dividers to create useable spaces. Immediately upon entry, he encountered a table and chairs that he could use for dining or as a desk space. Beyond that, partially obstructed by an ornate room divider, he saw the hint of a washroom. It would be simple, he knew. A basin and mirror were visible, but there might be some sort of hassock or compost toilet on the other side of that divider—a luxury Kotler was happy to have.

Water would be supplied in buckets, he was sure. He was tempted to clean up a bit, to wash his face and body before turning in, but he felt the need for sleep like an ache in his bones.

The space he was most concerned about was the "bedroom."

Another divider created an area to the right side of the tent, and Kotler made his way there, where he was sure to find a cot waiting for him.

He stopped short as he rounded the corner.

A man stood in the darkness of the space. In his hand was a weapon, trained on Kotler's chest.

"Dr. Kotler," the man said. "I am so pleased you have arrived."

CHAPTER SIX

Denzel had slept like the dead.

Not an expression he really cared for, but he couldn't deny the accuracy, after a night of deep and dreamless sleep. He had stumbled into the tent and dropped onto his cot, fully dressed and with his hand still on his bag, and had been asleep almost instantly. It wasn't until the morning that he learned he was sharing the tent with three other guys, all of whom had stirred only enough to witness his zombie-like collapse into oblivion.

It had made for a decent ice breaker, and they'd spent the early morning hours making introductions.

Now, as daybreak came a little too early, Denzel joined the others in milling around a table under the commissary tent, sipping coffee and eating a light breakfast of fruit and cereal.

There was a lot of chatter and excitement. Kotler was a hero here, and once people discovered that he and Denzel worked together, the questions wouldn't stop. It was annoying, but Denzel could understand it.

These were Kotler's people.

Of course everyone here respected him. He deserved it. He

had earned it. And in those moments when Denzel was being entirely honest with himself, he could admit that this bothered him.

For two years now he and Kotler had been partners, of a sort. Denzel was in charge of the FBI's new Historic Crimes Division, and had agents working under him to solve cases of an historical nature. His department was well funded, for what it was. He had a team of forensic specialists all his own, which was a rarity in the Bureau for sure. And his department occupied most of a whole floor of Manhattan's FBI offices, with case archives occupying the rest. This worked out well for the department, as their cases tended to rely on quick access to archived files and evidence. Half the archive space was filled with artifacts and objects that were integral to Historic Crimes cases.

Denzel managed people and resources, and helped to solve cases that had both historical ties and world-altering implications. But there was a part of him that wondered if it would all fall apart if Kotler left.

It was a petty thought, Denzel knew. Kotler was his friend, as well as his colleague. It would be selfish to want to keep him from doing work he was passionate about, just so he'd still be around. A true friend would want Kotler to move on, if he found something better, and Denzel absolutely wanted that for Kotler.

But he couldn't help feeling that if Kotler did leave Historic Crimes, he'd be running away, not moving forward.

Kotler had run before. Or withdrawn, at least. The past two years had been rough for him, Denzel knew, with friends dying and with the woman he loved betraying him. Things got bad at times. And more than once Kotler had taken a break from it all. He'd gone on speaking tours, and taken time to write and publish. He'd been part of several television productions, from around the world. And he'd often participated in work like this, excavating a tomb or dusting sand from some broken statue.

And every time, Denzel had appeared, a case in hand, asking Kotler to come back. And Kotler always had.

This time felt different.

Maybe it was how this dig site tied to Kotler's past, or the fact that he'd had such a significant and positive influence on Dr. Martook Maalyck, who clearly idolized (and flattered) him. Maybe it was the honor of having the Egyptian government and the Cairo museum officially ask him to lead this expedition. Or it could just be that the mystery of all this, the presence of Celtic mythology in Egypt, was too intriguing to resist. A mystery like that was a big draw for Kotler.

In a lot of ways, Denzel knew, this site was parallel to the one that started it all for the two of them—the dig site in Pueblo, Colorado, where a Viking presence had been discovered. Maybe Kotler saw this as a chance to pick the other road, to turn left instead of right and to get his old life back on track, now with new prestige and respect.

Whatever the reason, Denzel knew almost from the instant Maalyck had shown up that this was a strong temptation for Kotler. He played it as if he were coming here to make a final decision, but Denzel worried he would just take on the role and uproot his life and...

What, exactly? Regret it later?

Maybe. Or maybe that was just Denzel's own issue.

He had come along on this for his own reasons. If Kotler were going to leave Historic Crimes, Denzel wanted to know that he'd considered it from every angle. Maybe Denzel was just trying to see it all for himself, to know that Kotler was making the best decision. He certainly had no authority to force Kotler to come back to Historic Crimes, but at the very least he could be there for his friend, encourage him and offer advice, if he needed it. And, sure, maybe talk him into staying, if he could.

Selfish motives, maybe. Denzel didn't exactly have a play-book here.

They had been lingering under the commissary tent for a while, giving Kotler some leeway, thinking he must have over-slept. But as the clock ticked on, Denzel knew something was wrong.

He left the commons, and with a couple of people from the camp to guide him, he found his way to Kotler's tent.

"He gets this whole tent to himself?" Denzel asked, looking at the two researchers who had accompanied him. They stared back at him, blankly, and he shook his head. "Kotler, you in there?"

They waited, and when no answer came, Denzel exchanged looks with the researchers, then pushed into the tent.

There was no sign of him, inside.

Denzel moved around in the space, looking for signs and clues. When he rounded into the small, makeshift bedroom, he stopped.

On the floor, beside the still-made cot, was Kotler's bag. It was unopened, as if it had been tossed to that spot and Kotler had simply walked away.

There were no signs of a struggle.

Denzel turned to the researchers. "Go find Dr. Maalyck," he told one. And to the other, "Who's in charge of security here?"

The second researcher blinked. "There's a contingent of the Egyptian military," he said. "I don't know who's in charge of it."

"Find me someone," Denzel said.

They both hesitated, and Denzel shook his head, patting his shirt and pants pockets. His badge was in his bag, back in his tent. "I'm an FBI agent," he said. They again paused, mystified. "Go!"

They went, moving quickly out of the tent and leaving Denzel standing there, alone.

He turned, slowly. The space was enviably large, but there was no sign that Kotler had spent any time in it at all. Denzel would have to ask around, but he was pretty sure he knew the answers he'd get—that no one had seen Kotler since he was dropped off last night.

Sometime between Denzel saying goodnight to him and this morning, Kotler had just disappeared.

Denzel left the tent, grabbed someone passing by, and ordered them not to let anyone else in or out until he'd returned. He then rushed back to his own tent to retrieve his badge, which might help grease the wheels with the Egyptian military.

He wished to God he'd brought his gun.

CHAPTER SEVEN

KOTLER DID NOT KNOW his abductor, but he knew right away the man was an archeologist. Or, at any rate, he was someone who had studied in the field, and who held all the accoutrements of the role.

The room in which Kotler was being held was familiar for its details, if not for the space itself. Books on a range of topics lined almost every wall, and lay open on nearly every flat surface. Instruments of investigation—magnifying glass, small metal picks and probes, tiny brushes—were scattered on a work surface lined with a leather mat.

There were no computers or other electronics, which was not altogether surprising. This place felt like a throwback to an earlier time in archaeology. Or to the set of an *Indiana Jones* film. But the lack of a computer meant there was no opportunity for Kotler to make contact with the outside world. Mobile phone reception was spotty at best in this region, and regardless he didn't have his phone. And there would be no land line. The best he had hoped for was a satellite internet connection, as he would have had at the camp.

They had not traveled far from the research site, and might even be near the village. He couldn't be entirely sure.

Kotler had been forced into a truck, his hands and feet bound together by a length of chain, and they had bounced along through the pitch darkness for maybe an hour, though the timeline was difficult to gauge. The moon and stars had not been visible, and the truck had no clock. In fact, its dash was darkened to the point of being invisible. The only light came from the headlamps, illuminating the road and the canyon walls.

They had arrived at a house made of stone and adobe, with beams protruding from high on its exterior walls. A second story, and Kotler was led into the building and up the stairs, locked in this room with a trove of archaeological resources. The man, who had left him momentarily, had said nothing the entire time, other than brief commands.

Kotler had kept quiet, too. He could see from the man's body language that he was desperate, even fanatical. There was no indication of what he wanted, and no way to know what might trigger him.

Kotler had learned long ago that it was best to stay silent in the presence of fanatics, to let them tell you what they're after. *There's no reasoning with crazy*, his father once said, and it was a truism that stuck with Kotler all his life.

With his hands and feet still bound, and now locked to the chair he was sitting in, Kotler couldn't explore the room for resources. Instead, he scanned the room and took everything in, trying to learn as much about his captor as he could.

The man had left Kotler here alone, which meant he was confident Kotler couldn't escape. It also meant that if he shouted for help, he'd get no answer.

Kotler craned his neck to read the titles of the books that were open on the work surface. Open books meant they were current references. If Kotler could determine what the man was interested in, before being asked any questions, it might give him an advantage.

Some of the titles were written in Masry, the most common Egyptian language and one in which Kotler was fluent. These tended to be texts about the region and local history, with a bit of mythology and mysticism thrown in. Other books, on similar topics, were in Arabic. The majority of the books, however, were written in English. Almost all of them were references to ancient pantheons—accounts of the gods of other regions and cultures. Prominent among these titles was a book about the Irish deities, opened to a section about the *Tuatha dé Danann* and the Otherworld.

There was the sound of footsteps from the wooden stairs, and Kotler straightened, slumping as if he were exhausted and distraught by this ordeal. It wasn't much of an act, as Kotler still felt the fatigue from two days of hard travel. His adrenaline was compensating for some of that, but he could use a solid night of sleep.

The man entered the room, looking warily at Kotler, as if worried that he may have slipped his bonds. Apparently satisfied that all was safe, the man stood in front of Kotler, looking down on him.

"You are the great Dr. Kotler. Discoverer of the brass hall of Credne."

Kotler wasn't sure what response the man wanted, but as he wasn't currently holding a gun on him, he decided to go with his instinct.

"I'm afraid you have me mixed up with someone else," Kotler said in a dry tone.

The man blinked. "You are not Dr. Kotler?"

"My name is Agent Roland Denzel," Kotler said. "I'm with the FBI."

The man shook his head, turning away from Kotler and pacing near his workstation. "That is impossible," he muttered. He stood in front of the open book about the *Tuatha dé*, and Kotler had to turn his head uncomfortably to see him.

"You know the penalty for abducting a US Federal agent, don't you?" Kotler said. "Life imprisonment, at best. In the deepest hole we can find. You'll never see your home country again."

He was playing a heavy hand and decided he should pull back a little. He wasn't entirely sure about this man's mental stability, or his level of knowledge about US law enforcement. It was clear he was Egyptian, and well educated. Kotler needed to make sure he didn't overstep.

The man turned to him, and Kotler saw signs of zeal in his body language. The set of his jaw, the glint in his eyes, the squaring of his shoulders. This had just gone wrong.

"I do not believe you," he said. "You are Dr. Kotler. You discovered the brass hall of Credne. And you will help me open the door to the Otherworld. Or you will die."

CHAPTER EIGHT

"WE UNDERSTAND YOUR CONCERNS," said the Ra'id—the Egyptian equivalent to the rank of Captain, in the US military. Ra'id Medo Sarraf did not, in Denzel's estimate, seem the least bit interested in his concerns. He seemed more perturbed at having his morning interrupted, and with having a US agent present. "We will do all we can to find your missing man. But you must understand that you have no official presence here, Agent Denzel."

Denzel nodded. "That's true. But I would greatly appreciate it if you'd allow me to help in the search, or at least keep me apprised of what you're finding. Dr. Kotler is a good friend of mine."

Sarraf studied Denzel for a moment and then nodded. "Certainly. As long as you do not interfere."

Denzel knew that was code for "we're in charge." Which was fine, as long as they were actually doing something.

Sarraf turned and gave orders to two of his men, speaking in Masry. Denzel didn't understand the words, but he understood the tone. He'd gotten the score from Sarraf when he and his men had first arrived.

People went missing in this region all the time. There could be any number of reasons why a man would wander from his tent in the middle of the night. There were prostitutes in the village, for example. Or he may have been taken for ransom. If he were found alive at all, it was likely one of these things.

What troubled Denzel was that he could practically smell the corruption among Sarraf and his men. There was no guarantee that they hadn't been paid to look the other way, as Kotler was taken. They might even have assisted in his abduction, for the right price.

Denzel would have to keep an eye on these men. And that was attention he couldn't spare.

After leaving Sarraf and the others, Denzel found Maalyck.

The young researcher seemed distraught but was holding things together. He was doing an excellent job of keeping the work going, keeping the researchers on task, and ensuring the site remained operational. It was clear he was a skilled manager of resources.

"Any word?" Maalyck asked.

Denzel shook his head. "And to be honest, I'm not hopeful. I think we'll have to work this out ourselves." He looked around the camp. It was now late in the day, and people were busy with their various tasks. In the hills surrounding them, there had been carved a number of paths, and people moved to and from various sites in the mountainside. Some carried artifacts with them, bringing them to the camp for closer study or to run tests.

Denzel turned to Maalyck. "Kotler has enemies, but this doesn't feel like it's about him, exactly. That's just gut instinct on my part, especially since we really don't know anything. But let's start with right here and now. Do you know any reason why someone local would want to abduct Dr. Kotler?"

Maalyck considered the question, then shook his head. "Whoever did this came into the camp, into Dr. Kotler's own tent. It is possible he was taken to be ransomed, but this sort of boldness is not typical here. People are abducted from the streets, in seclusion, usually as they walk alone. To come into the camp here means the abductor was bold and resourceful."

"And familiar with this site," Denzel said, thinking.

Maalyck nodded. "You are implying that it was someone from the research site."

"It has the earmarks of an inside job," Denzel said. "Whoever took him knew he'd be here, and when. They moved in and out of the camp without anyone taking notice."

"It is not so difficult," Maalyck replied, "to do such a thing. Security here can be bought, at the right price. But I tend to agree with your assessment, Agent Denzel. As much as it pains me, it does seem as though someone from this site is responsible."

"Would you be able to compile a list of possible suspects?" Denzel asked. "People who might have a grudge against Kotler? Or who might have some other motive for taking him?"

"I will do my best," Maalyck replied.

Denzel nodded, thinking. "Are there any cameras in the site?"

Maalyck shook his head. "Regrettably, no. Though there is now a strong case for them to be installed. However, there are cameras on the gateways to the sites, along the mountain's edge. These are maintained by the Egyptian military."

Denzel considered this. "Can you get that footage? Maybe from the last twenty-four hours? It's at least a lead to pursue."

"I will make the request," Maalyck nodded.

They chatted a few minutes more, and Denzel left,

returning to Kotler's tent. It was one of the few private spaces in the camp, and Denzel had commandeered it to be his HQ while they searched for clues about Kotler's abduction. It helped, he would admit, that he could crash on Kotler's bunk when he needed to, away from the snoring and chatting of his tent-mates. But of greater value was having space to set up for a proper investigation. Denzel used the table as a desk for his laptop, and he could work in private here.

There was also the advantage of a satellite connection that allowed Denzel to get online, and to tap into some of his resources back in Manhattan. There wasn't much to go on, yet, but as more information came in it would be helpful to have at least partial access to his team.

He took a moment to update Liz Ludlum on the situation, in an email that he hoped sounded reassuring. It was early morning in New York, and there was a chance that Ludlum would get his email any minute. He'd do a video call with her later, and answer any questions she had. He might need her help, as well. She was smart, and had a pretty good head for piecing together details. Denzel had been impressed with her, during the ordeal with Dr. Robert Wiley and the assassin, Red Ryba. She'd shown herself to be incredibly competent and capable, well above and beyond her duties as the Lead Forensic Specialist.

Of course, she also had a romantic relationship with Kotler. Which did complicate things. Technically, there was no rule against it, since Kotler was a consultant and not a Bureau employee. But that wouldn't prevent some challenges and diffi-culties, if something went south in their relationship. It was something Denzel tried to keep an eye on without interfering.

Still, he had to let her know what was going on with Kotler.

About two hours after his conversation with Maalyck, someone called to him through the tent's front flap, and Denzel bade them come inside. One of the researchers brought him a thumb drive containing video surveillance for each of the gated paths, from the past twenty-four hours.

Denzel thanked them and got to work, scrubbing through videos one by one as fast as he could manage. He noted anything that seemed anomalous, but so far was having very little luck. There was just too much footage to go through.

This was going to take too long. Or, worse, he might miss something by hurrying. He would need to think of a new approach.

He copied the files to a cloud server and sent them to his team back in the states, with a note that he needed them analyzed as quickly as possible. He would continue to scan through them himself, but he felt much better knowing he had backup.

The day was starting to fade toward night, and Denzel wasn't sure they'd made much progress. Wherever Kotler was, Denzel prayed he was ok. He knew Kotler was resourceful, and if he could he would find a way to get a message out. Or to escape.

Denzel counted on this, letting it convince him enough that he could put his mind on the tasks at hand.

Kotler could take care of himself.

CHAPTER NINE

THE MAN DROPPED a book into Kotler's lap. It landed front-cover down, and on the back was a photo of Kotler, along with his name and bio.

The jig was up.

"You are Dr. Kotler, the anthropologist. You and Martook Maalyck discovered the brass hall, twenty years ago."

Kotler said nothing.

The man lunged at him, gripping his shirt and pushing his face close. Flecks of spittle hit Kotler's face as the man shouted. "You are Dr. Kotler!"

Kotler had turned his face slightly, and winced from the sudden attack, but nodded. "It's me," he said. "I'm Dr. Kotler."

The man stayed close to Kotler's face for a long while, studying him, his eyes wide. And then, as if the answer he'd gotten had been some sort of antipsychotic drug, the man calmed, stood straight, even smoothed Kotler's shirt.

"I am sorry," he said, for all the world as if he'd merely bumped into Kotler by accident. "It is very important to me that you are honest."

"I can see that," Kotler said.

The man took a handkerchief out of his pocket and used it to wipe at Kotler's face, for which Kotler was half grateful.

"I am Dr. Ammon Cairo ELsayed," he said. "Known as Ammon."

The name wasn't familiar to Kotler, but he did note that *Ammon* was Egyptian for "the hidden." No real significance to the fact, but it seemed ominous nonetheless.

"For some years, I was a researcher at the Credne site, working directly with Dr. Joseph Warner."

"You've ... come a long way," Kotler said cautiously, but unable to help himself.

Ammon didn't appear to notice. "For many years I was Dr. Warner's protege. We worked very closely together. He did not care for you."

Kotler shook his head. "No, we never got along."

"You were not a true academic," Ammon said, and there was that hint of zeal in his voice again, as if he had just proclaimed Kotler a heretic to the faith of academia.

"I have no university affiliation," Kotler replied, opting to be cautious but honest. "I'm an independent."

Ammon sneered. "*Independent.*" He moved around in the space, adjusting items on some of the work surfaces, nudging the spines of books with his index finger. Kotler watched him, wondering if he might become violent over this. Anything could be a provocation to an unsettled mind.

Ammon stopped in front of a table and shook his head. He picked up a blade, about eighteen inches long. It had no handle, but that wouldn't prevent it from piercing Kotler's flesh if Ammon gave it the right amount of thrust.

Ammon brought the bade closer, standing over Kotler. "A few years ago, your friend Martook Maalyck returned from University. He had his choice of any research site in the world, but he chose to come here. He and Dr. Warner worked very closely together."

Was that what this was about? Professional rivalry between Maalyck and Ammon? Kotler had seen that sort of thing get out of hand, but there was more to this than Ammon was telling.

"Because of Maalyck's involvement at the Credne site, I was transferred from my duties. This was ... unfortunate." At this Ammon lifted the blade, studying it. Kotler could envision Ammon thrusting the blade into his throat, but tried to keep that sort of thought at bay. He needed to stay calm, to think. Ammon was giving him useful information, and there might be something that Kotler could use.

Ammon locked eyes with Kotler. "I was so very close, Dr. Kotler. But Dr. Warner ... it was not fast enough. I was not fast enough."

"Warner could be impatient," Kotler offered, hoping to find some common ground with this man.

It backfired.

"Dr. Warner was a genius!" Ammon shouted, and in a flash, the blade was pointed at Kotler's throat.

There was a pause, and Ammon slowly backed away, lowering the blade to his side. "A genius," he repeated. "And we were close to a discovery. I believe we could have solved it, if Maalyck had simply stayed away. But he was here. He came here and the direction of inquiry changed. He was the golden child of the University. Top of his class. Sought after, even before doing his first official project. He already had a reputation, you know. Before entering the University."

"I've learned that," Kotler said.

Ammon held the blade up again. "It was because of Maalyck that I was forced to make this."

Kotler studied the blade for the first time, not just as his potential cause of death but as an artifact. What he saw surprised him.

Etched into the blade were Celtic symbols, and Kotler recognized them immediately. "Is that ... did you make a replica of the bronze sword?"

Ammon smiled. "The sword of Credne. Retrieved by you and Maalyck, as the mountain collapsed around the brass hall. It was a story I heard often. Maalyck was insufferable in his admiration for you."

Kotler said nothing to this, for fear of provoking Ammon regardless of his answer.

Ammon laughed, and then tossed the blade onto a nearby work surface. "It is useless, however. A perfect replica, and yet it did not work. I need the real sword."

Things finally clicked for Kotler. "You're trying to enter Credne's tomb."

Ammon nodded. "The door to the Otherworld." He indicated the blade with a nod. "The sword is the key. But I must have gotten something wrong. The cast I used was perfect, but perhaps there was some flaw I did not see." He got quiet for a moment. He spoke again in a half-mumble, as if talking to himself. "Perhaps it was the weight. Without the hilt, there is only the weight of the blade ..."

Kotler used the opportunity to look around again, cautiously taking in the details of the room in light of this new information.

It was clear that Ammon was unstable, but he did appear to have moments of lucidity. That could be the only thing keeping Kotler alive, but it might change at any moment.

He needed to find a way out of here.

With his hands and feet bound by chains, there was no real hope of making a run for it. His best plan would be to take Ammon by surprise somehow, maybe use a weapon. The blade? It was the focus of Ammon's attention, impossible to reach without being noticed. But there were other objects in the room that might be just as effective.

Ammon suddenly turned and bent over Kotler, his eyes narrowing and his voice intense. "You will help me to retrieve the real key, and to enter Credne's tomb. You will help me to reach the Otherworld."

Kotler studied Ammon's face. There was more than just fanaticism there. The man was intelligent. Whatever was driving him, though, was something akin to religious zeal. The Otherworld had become a real place to him, a destination he would reach even if it cost him everything.

That sort of obsession made him even more dangerous.

"Ammon," Kotler said, cautiously. "I don't know how to reach the Otherworld. I can't help you."

"You will help by being a bartering chip," Ammon smiled, standing straight. "Maalyck will hand over the sword to get you back. He will have no choice."

Kotler shook his head. "Your government will never allow that."

"Maalyck will convince them. Or he will betray them. It makes no difference to me." He turned then, leaving Kotler for a moment. When he returned, he had a video camera in his hand.

"You will repeat what I tell you," Ammon said. "Word for word."

LIZ LUDLUM GOT Denzel's email late in the afternoon.

It had been a busy day, and she hadn't had a moment to check until now. Her inbox had a filter that prioritized certain senders, however, and Denzel's was at the top. She read through it, felt her heart drop into her stomach, and immediately tried a video call.

It would be very late in Egypt. Or very early, depending on one's point of view. The eight-hour time difference meant it would be after midnight at the camp.

Still, she doubted Denzel would be sleeping.

She made several attempts, and after nearly half an hour Denzel finally answered. He looked a bit tired, but he was fully dressed, and showed no signs of having been asleep.

"Any word?" Ludlum asked immediately, trying to keep her voice neutral.

Denzel shook his head. It was dark where he was, and the space behind him disappeared into shadow. His face was lit by an electric lantern that Ludlum could see just at the edge of the frame.

"We're reviewing security footage, but so far no luck. I have the team on it, there in Manhattan. We'll find him, Liz."

"Do we know why he was taken?" she asked. She was in her analytic mode now, emotionally neutral, considering facts and asking questions.

It was keeping her from panicking.

"No note, no message. No sign of struggle. Nothing," Denzel said.

Ludlum considered this. "They took him from his own tent? In the middle of that camp? Where was security?"

"Security is a little ... relaxed, here. It's more about protecting the site and the artifacts than the people. Though supposedly the Ra'id is stepping up measures. I think that's because I'm here, honestly. He doesn't like having an American Federal Agent on site."

Ludlum huffed, not sure what to say or do. Worry was starting to crack her professional facade. She shook her head. "What can I do to help?"

Denzel considered for a moment. "I could use a single point of contact for anything happening there. Agent Brown is handling day-to-day operations for the department, while I'm out. It would be helpful if you coordinated with the team on their findings, make sure nothing gets lost or left out."

She nodded. "Of course. I'll talk to Danielle in a moment, let her know what's happening. I'll also alert my forensics team so they can cover for me."

Denzel nodded. He paused, looked uncomfortable, but said, "We're going to find him. He's going to be ok."

Ludlum also nodded. "I know. He can take care of himself. He always does."

They ended the call, and Ludlum went to Denzel's office, where Agent Danielle Brown had taken up temporary residence. Ludlum knocked on the door frame, and Brown looked up from her work and motioned her in.

She gestured for Ludlum to sit as she finished typing something, then she looked up, smiling slightly, but her expression making it plain she knew what this was about. "How are you?"

Ludlum shook her head. "I only just found out. But I'm fine. Agent Denzel asked me to be the liaison between him and our team here."

Brown nodded. "He mentioned that he needed someone. And you're covered, in the lab?"

Ludlum nodded. "I'll make arrangements."

Brown watched her for a moment, then sighed. "I know you and Dr. Kotler are ... close. But can I ask you something?"

Ludlum's expression was curious.

"Have you noticed how often Kotler ends up in the middle of something like this? The abductions. Firefights. Sociopaths who make threats on a super villain level. And somehow ..."
She stopped short.

"Somehow what?" Ludlum asked.

"Somehow, Kotler is the one who always ends up solving the whole thing."

Ludlum studied her for a moment. "And you think that's suspicious?"

"You don't?" Brown asked.

Ludlum considered what she was saying, turning again to that analytical habit that had been her guide and instinct for so many years. She thought of everything she knew about Kotler, about Historic Crimes, and about the cases the FBI had allowed Denzel to work over the past two years.

She had to admit, it was pretty incredible.

"Fortune favors the bold," Brown said.

Ludlum looked up. "What?"

"It's an old adage. Good luck tends to fall in the lap of the people brave enough to take chances. I think the same sort of idea might apply to Kotler. Maybe a little in reverse. These things keep happening to him because he keeps leaping into it. Trouble finds Kotler because he goes looking for it, maybe. Either that, or there's some shadowy government conspiracy." She said this last with a sort of mysterious voice, waving her fingers as if to indicate secrecy and mysticism.

She laughed, and Ludlum felt relieved for some reason.

"Anyway, I'm glad to hear Agent Denzel has recruited you for this. I was already drowning a little," she indicated the laptop in front of her, as well as stacks of file folders on the desk.

Ludlum shook her head and stood. "Sorry, yes. I know you're busy. If I can help ..."

"You're already helping," Brown smiled. "Let me know if you need anything."

Ludlum left and made her way down the stairs to the main floor. She wandered across to the glass doors leading to the

Forensics labs. Before opening the door, she caught a glimpse of a reflection.

It was getting late, the sun had dipped below the skyline, and it was just dark enough that the details of the Historic Crimes offices were visible in the reflection. And so Ludlum could clearly see Agent Brown, standing in the doorway of Denzel's office, watching her.

Ludlum swiped her badge through the reader and opened the door to her labs, stepping inside without looking back. Once she was beyond the sight line of the exterior offices, she stopped and turned. No one was visible from this angle.

She shook her head, continuing on to her own lab She had emails to send and calls to make. She needed to make some arrangements. And above all, she needed to help find Kotler.

Somehow he seemed to be in more danger now than ever.

CHAPTER TEN

KOTLER'S FACE appeared on the laptop, as Denzel and Maalyck watched.

The video had arrived several minutes ago, in an envelope addressed to Maalyck. He had watched only a few seconds before calling for Denzel.

"My name is Dr. Dan Kotler. I am being held against my will. My life is being threatened. My abductors require a ransom for my safe return, and will only accept the sword of Credne in exchange for my life."

"The sword?" Maalyck repeated, shaking his head.

Kotler's message continued. "Dr. Martook Maalyck, alone, is required to bring the sword to the coordinates included with the thumb drive."

Maalyck showed Denzel the envelope in which the thumb drive had been delivered, indicating a set of hand-written coordinates under Maalyck's name.

"My abductor will be able to authenticate the sword instantly, so do not attempt to deliver a replica. He will also know if the Egyptian authorities have been contacted, and will kill me instantly.

"Dr. Maalyck will deliver the sword to the coordinates within 24 hours and return to the camp. He will bring no police or security, and no one from the camp will accompany him. If these instructions are not followed, I will be executed. The time is indicated on this video. The clock starts now."

Kotler's eyes flicked offscreen, and when he looked back he said, "Please tell Gail that I'll be alright, and we'll still take that trip to Antarctica. I hope she still has the map."

The video ended abruptly then, and Denzel straightened.

Maalyck was shaking his head. "My government, the museum—they will never allow me to give this person the sword."

"No," Denzel said. "I think they know that. They said not to involve the authorities. They probably mean for you to steal the sword and deliver it to them."

He thought for a moment, considering Kotler's final statement.

Tell Gail that I'll be alright.

That, and the reference to Antarctica were clearly meant as some sort of coded message.

"He mentioned the map," Denzel said.

"A trip to Antarctica does not sound like a suitably romantic getaway," Maalyck said. "Is it a perhaps a clue to his location?"

Denzel shook his head. "That isn't it. He said to tell Gail he'd be alright. Gail McCarthy died in Antarctica. She was the head of an international smuggling ring. They did have a relationship, at one point, but she betrayed him." He thought about this. "I think that was part of the message. Betrayal. I think that was meant to indicate it's someone you know."

Maalyck considered this. "So it is true," he said. "Someone in this camp is responsible."

"Maybe," Denzel said. "There may be more to the message that will help us narrow that down. Kotler said that whoever has him will be able to authenticate the sword. That implies they have some familiarity with it, right?"

Maalyck nodded. "Very few members of this team have directly studied the sword."

"Get me a list," Denzel said. He thought for a moment. "He mentioned the map ..." his trailed off.

"What is significant about this map?" Maalyck asked. "It is a map of Antarctica?"

"It was a fake. A forgery." Denzel looked up. "But still a map, leading us to what we were after. A map within a map, hidden in plain sight."

Again, Maalyck nodded. "This person wants the sword. They must also know its purpose, to open the tomb of Credne."

"But they don't know about the map," Denzel said. "That's what Kotler is trying to tell us. They want the key, but they don't realize there's a map, hidden in plain sight. They don't know about the pommel."

"How does this information help us?" Maalyck asked.

Denzel shook his head. "I'm not sure yet, but any time you have an advantage over an enemy, you should press it. Kotler was giving us a way to get the upper hand on this guy. We know what he's after, more or less. He'll need to gain access to that chamber, with the face ..."

"The face of Credne," Maalyck offered.

"Yeah, that one. So now we know that whoever this is, they've also been in that chamber. They know about the face and the gateway and all of that. Does that help us narrow things down any?"

Maalyck was thinking. He took a notepad from the table

and began jotting names. When he was done, there was a list of ten. "These are all the people who, to my knowledge, would be aware of both the sword and the face of Credne, as well as have access to the translations."

Denzel took the list and looked it over. "Any way we can narrow this down?"

Maalyck thought, then scratched through two of the names. "Dr. Warner, of course, has passed away."

Denzel nodded. "Ok, good. What about the second name?"

Maalyck shook his head. "Dr. Grace Tennant. She left the project after Dr. Warner's death. I am still in touch with her. She is the lead at a site in Brittany, in north-western France. She knew of the sword and its history, and she was one of the researchers who helped in the discovery of the chamber and the translations."

"It's still possible she could be involved," Denzel said, stretching. He was tired, and he needed a hot meal almost as much as he needed sleep. "Could we get her on a video call? Interview her, to eliminate her as a suspect?"

Maalyck nodded. "I can make arrangements."

Denzel nodded. "Ok, and I'd like to chat with the rest of the people on this list. But we have a limited amount of time here." He paused. "We need that sword."

Maalyck shook his head. "As I have said, the government and the museum would never allow it."

"Dr. Maalyck, Kotler's life is in jeopardy. I wouldn't ask this if I could think of a way to avoid it, but if this person really can authenticate that sword on sight, then it's our only bargaining chip."

Maalyck was clearly distressed over this. "If it is discovered, I could be imprisoned. At best, my career would be finished."

He didn't mention the worst case scenario, but they both

knew what it was. Imprisonment could be a fate worse than death, in this region.

"I do know what this could cost you," Denzel said. "Believe it or not, I face the same fate. I'm acting well outside my jurisdiction here. But I will risk that to make sure Kotler is returned safely. It's not fair to ask you to do the same, but I'm asking anyway."

Maalyck was quiet for a moment, then nodded. "I will do this. For Dr. Kotler."

Denzel smiled and nodded. "Good. But we don't have to give them the whole enchilada."

Maalyck shook his head. "I am sorry, I do not know this word."

"Forget it. What I mean is, we don't have to give them both the sword and the pommel. I think that's what Kotler was trying to tell me. This person is after whatever is behind that door, but they don't yet know about the map in the jewel. That gives us an advantage."

Maalyck grinned. "And when you have an advantage over an enemy, you must press it!"

Denzel smiled and nodded. "Exactly."

"This is a good enchilada," Maalyck nodded, sagely.

"No ... that's not ..."

"Shall we begin to vet the rest of the list?" Maalyck asked.

Denzel hesitated, then sighed and nodded again. "Let's do it. Maybe we can solve this before the clock is up, and you won't have to risk going to prison."

"This would be most welcome," Maalyck said, and turned to his laptop, arranging for the interviews.

"Focus on anyone you think might have a grudge against you," Denzel added.

"Me?" Maalyck responded, looking up.

"Whoever is behind this took Kotler as a bargaining chip

against you," Denzel said. "That means they know the history between the two of you, and they're using your relationship as leverage."

Maalyck consider. "You are right. I will prioritize the list in this way."

Denzel nodded and then left Maalyck's tent, returning to Kotler's, and thinking about all of this as he walked. They were pushing it, spending their twenty-four hours talking to people in the camp. At any time, whoever had Kotler could change their mind, get spooked, decide he was too much trouble.

It was all Denzel had, at the moment. He was short on leads.

"Keep cool, Kotler," Denzel whispered under his breath. "I'll get you out of this, somehow."

CHAPTER ELEVEN

AFTER KOTLER HAD FINISHED RECITING what he was told to say on the video, Ammon had forced him to his feet and down the stairs, out of the building and into the truck. It was brighter out now, about mid-day by Kotler's estimate, but that hardly helped matters. Kotler still had no idea where he was, and no means of escaping the chains binding his wrists and ankles.

They drove in silence. Kotler studied the landscape as they went, hoping for any clues that might be helpful, but there was precious little beyond mountains and desert soil. Even plant life was sparse here. And as far as Kotler could determine, there might not be a soul within a thousand miles.

They rattled through a canyon, and then stopped. Ammon came around to Kotler's side of the truck, and hauled him out, nearly causing Kotler to fall to the ground.

"There," Ammon pointed.

Kotler followed his gesture and saw that several feet away was a small cave, nestled behind a large boulder. Kotler hobbled to it, moving as best he could. The chains hindered his movements, making him slow and clumsy. Even if an opportunity arose, he couldn't run.

He was in serious trouble.

Inside the cave, Ammon told him to stand to the side. He stooped and unlocked the chains around Kotler's ankles, and used the length that ran between Kotler's feet and his wrists to lead Kotler to a metal ring in the wall. He chained Kotler to this.

"Now we wait. I will return with the sword."

"And then you'll set me free?" Kotler asked.

Ammon said nothing, but left the cave. Moments later Kotler heard the sound of the truck starting, and then the crunch of gravel as Ammon drove away.

Then, silence.

Kotler looked around the space, hoping to spot something, anything, that he might use as a tool to free himself. The cave was a natural gap in the stone, however. There was nothing here but rocks and what looked like the remains of a campfire. A squatter's camp, used as a temporary respite from walking through the mountains. It was difficult to tell how long it had been since anyone else had been here, and there were no signs of tools or weapons or anything else of use.

Kotler turned his attention to the ring in the wall.

His hands were in large shackles that covered his wrists almost two inches from his palms. There had been similar shackles on his ankles, but these now drooped from the ring in the wall, held in place by a thick, steel lock, dangling from a loop of chain that ran through the ring. There was a length of chain, about three feet, that allowed Kotler some range of motion, but not much. If he pulled it tight and stretched his arms, he could stand just short of the fire pit. There was nothing else in this space that provided any hope.

What were his options?

Studying the chain, he thought there could be the possibility of severing one of the links, maybe by smashing it with a stone.

It was worth a shot. The nearest stone with half a chance of being useful was in the ring of the fire pit, and so Kotler stretched to get as close as possible. He began fishing with his toe, trying to kick and pull one of the stones loose, to inch it a bit closer.

It was maddening how slow the process was, but in time he made some progress. He managed to hook the toe of his boot into a gap between two stones, and leverage this to nudge a stone in his direction.

Several more tries, and several more minutes, and he was able to scoot the stone close enough that he could kneel and pick it up. It had been a chore, but he suddenly felt a rush of adrenaline, over his success.

He used that as fuel.

The weak point would be the ring in the wall. He had no idea how deep the rod welded to that ring might penetrate into the stone, but judging by its firmness, he guessed it was in there pretty solid. Still, it presented him with a good target, much easier to strike than any link on the chain.

For the next hour, he slammed the stone into the ring, hit after hit, using all the strength he could manage. It was punishing work, taking a toll on him. He was tired and hadn't eaten in more than a day. His head hurt from the exertion. Still, he hammered down, hoping each time that he might snap the ring free, or otherwise open a gap he could exploit.

The steel stubbornly resisted his blows, and though it showed signs of damage, there was nothing to suggest it was any weaker now than when Kotler began.

He stopped, huffing, taking a breather.

His hands were raw from gripping the stone, and his arms

and shoulders and neck ached from the repeated strikes. There was a chance that even if he managed to break the ring, he might not be in any shape to make his escape. Still, there were no other options. This was his card, and he had to play it.

He let the stone drop and slumped to the floor, leaning against the wall, huffing.

There was still light coming in from outside, for which Kotler was grateful. He knew it was late in the day, that night was approaching. He wasn't sure what he would do, once night fell and his visibility dropped to zero.

It would get painfully cold here, once it was dark. Kotler's clothes would be enough to keep him from dying of hypothermia—he hoped—but it was going to be a long and uncomfortable night. He would have to fight numbness in his extremities, which would hamper his work.

Maybe he could start a fire.

He was too far away from the fire pit to really use it properly, but he might be able to drag some useful materials out of it. He could see scraps of wood, a few short limbs that were only half burned. He could scrape these with the rock to make some tinder, which would be easier to light, and kindle a fire with the remains.

All he needed was a way to ignite it.

First things first. He stretched himself across the space again and reached out with a foot to start kicking through the ash and small limbs in the fire pit. He began to nudge these out and toward himself. It was slow progress, and he worried for the time and the light he was wasting, but a pile of useable fuel was beginning to grow.

And then his foot struck something hard in the ash.

It wasn't a stone. It was long and thin. Kotler felt at its edges with his toe and then began working at it, dragging it closer. After a lot of effort, he heard the sound of metal scraping stone.

His heart pounded.

A short, metal rod. Likely something that was used as a fire poker, left behind by a former tenant of this cave. Kotler doubled his efforts, and after a bit of struggle, he managed to slide the rod up and over one of the remaining stones in the fire pit. It clanged to the stone floor of the cave, and from there Kotler managed to draw it closer, until he could stoop and pick it up.

It was an iron rod, possibly a piece of rebar, rusted and blackened with ash, but still sturdy.

He turned back to the ring in the wall.

His work with the stone had done some damage to the steel ring, but it would still take hours to smash his way through, if that were even possible. Now, though, he had a new resource.

He wedged the rod into the ring and angled it so that he could put pressure on the damaged metal. He then put all his weight into prying at the ring.

To his surprise, rather than break or even bend the ring, there was a snap, and he managed to make it turn in the wall.

Bits of stone from the surface of the wall chipped away as he did this, and Kotler could see in the dwindling light that his day's work had made some progress after all. The repeated slamming of the rock on the ring had managed to create cracks in the stone of the cave wall, loosening its grip on the shaft of the ring. Using the metal rod, he was able to turn the ring, which now moved freely in the wall.

Kotler changed his tactics.

He used the rod as a lever to pull at the ring, rather than turn it. In strong and sudden jerks, with a foot braced against the cave wall for leverage, Kotler worked the ring out bit by bit. After several strong tugs, the shaft of the ring gave way, pulling out of the wall and sending Kotler sprawling backward onto the ground.

He blinked, unsure of what had just happened despite hoping for it for the past several minutes.

He was free.

Or, he was untethered, at least.

He quickly got to his feet and gathered the chain, draping it over his shoulder. He held the metal rod in his right hand, ready to use it as a weapon.

It wasn't ideal. The chain was heavy, and it would encumber him, especially as he made his way through the mountains in the pitch black of the night. But his odds were better out there than in here, by his estimate. He might find a way to remove the chain, maybe stumble across someone who could help him or at least let him use tools.

He was willing to take the risk. Staying here would be suicide.

He made his way quickly out of the cave, into the Egyptian night. To his relief, the skies above were so clear, and there was so little ambient light here, that he could see the stars perfectly. Not only did this give him something of a psychological boost, but it served a practical purpose. He could determine his direction and set a course. He had no way of knowing where the research camp was, in relation to his current position. And he didn't know if there were any other towns or villages nearby. But he did know the general direction in which Ammon had taken him. He would use that, as a start.

He began his march, chains rattling and metal rod in hand. He wasn't sure who, but he felt like he must resemble some literary character. Jacob Marley, perhaps, bearing the chains he forged in life.

It wasn't a comforting thought, and Kotler wished he hadn't made the connection. But it did help drive him forward.

The last thing he intended to do was to die out here.

CHAPTER TWELVE

DENZEL HAD ELIMINATED MOST of Maalyck's list now, but was no closer to finding Kotler. The clock was counting down, and they were short on leads.

Maalyck had prioritized the list, as best he could, placing anyone who might have a grudge against him at the top. Denzel had interviewed these people first—a process that had been a frustrating strain on time. Many of these researchers were either onsite or otherwise indisposed, and had to be hunted down. In many cases, Maalyck had to intervene and insist that they cooperate.

This made things tricky. Everyone in camp knew that Kotler had been abducted, and so it was expected there would be some inquiry. Denzel was playing it careful, being cautious with the potential grudge matches. He didn't want to spook the abductor, which might cause them to run. But it was taking too much time.

If he could operate under his full authority, as a Federal Agent, things might be different. But that authority was a thin veil here, practically non-existent. Denzel had little choice but to continue to work through the channels and resources at his disposal, banking on voluntary cooperation even under the pressure of the clock.

The latest interview hadn't gotten him anywhere, and he was making notes as they left.

"Mr. Denzel," a woman said from the flap of the tent. He'd kept it open, throwing some natural daylight into the space but also inviting anyone with information to feel free to come in and share. An "open door policy" for the desert, he figured.

"Dr. Maalyck says that Dr. Tennant will call you within the next few minutes. He's spoken to her."

"Thank you," Denzel said.

The woman nodded and left, and Denzel opened his laptop. A moment later the app alerted him to a call, and he turned on video.

The woman onscreen was maybe a little younger than Denzel, and was thin and fit looking. Attractive, Denzel thought, but what seemed most striking about her was the look in her eyes. Even translated over the video call, she looked as if she were perpetually curious. He could see the intelligence in her expression, and it reminded him of someone. He couldn't quite place who.

"Dr. Tennant?"

She smiled. "Yes. And you're Agent Denzel?" Her accent was British, though Denzel wasn't sure what region of the UK she might be from.

Denzel nodded. "Thank you for taking the time to speak with me."

"No, it's fine," she said. "Dr. Maalyck told me about Dr. Kotler's abduction. I'm very sorry to hear it. How can I help?"

"Mostly I'm trying to clear everyone who knew about both the sword and the Credne chamber. You've been in France this whole time, is that correct?"

She nodded, her lips pursed in a smile. "Oh yes. There are hundreds of people who can verify that. I am the lead at this site. I've been in perpetual meetings for months," she laughed lightly at this, finally sighing. "I'm afraid I won't be much help. I haven't returned to the Credne site since Dr. Warren passed."

"You knew Dr. Warren well?" Denzel asked.

"Very," she replied. "I worked with him directly."

"And when Dr. Maalyck arrived, did you feel any animosity toward him?"

She laughed. "No, none whatsoever. I rather like Dr. Maalyck. He's remarkable. Quite talented. And endearing. He ... well, not to put too fine a point on it, he came into the field somewhat disadvantaged by a lack of basic education. But perhaps what makes him so charming is that he worked so hard to overcome this liability. He studied independently, read voraciously, and pursued this career with a brilliant single-mindedness. I quite admire him."

Denzel noted Tennant's statements. It certainly seemed as though she were being honest, and legitimately respected Maalyck. He decided to take another tack.

"Was there anyone in the camp who didn't like Maalyck?"

She made a noise, something between a scoff and a laugh. "Oh yes. Many," she said. "Prejudice often runs rampant at sites such as these."

"Was there anyone in particular?" Denzel asked. "Anyone who held a notable grudge?"

She nodded. "I would say that Ammon fits that description quite well. He despised Dr. Maalyck."

"Ammon?" Denzel asked. He checked the list and saw no one by that name.

"My apologies. Dr. Ammon Cairo ELsayed," Tennant said. Her expression shifted as she said his name, and it was plain she wasn't a fan. "He worked directly with Dr. Warren as well, and was not at all pleased when Dr. Maalyck chose to return to the Credne site. His connection to the original discovery made him somewhat famous among the researchers. Dr. Warren had led the research at the site all those years ago and remembered Martook—Dr. Maalyck—as a sort of pest, but he was pleased to see him become such a dedicated anthropologist."

"So this person, Ammon, was jealous of Maalyck? Did he lose his position?"

She nodded. "To a point, yes. Ammon had unofficially become Dr. Warren's right-hand man. He was born in the region, though to a wealthier family. He received his primary education in Cairo and continued on to University there. Dr. Warren appreciated his perspective on the site, in light of local culture. Martook had a much deeper insight, however, as someone who was born and raised in the village nearby. He knew the terrain intimately, and it was he who led Dr. Kotler to discover the brass hall of Credne."

She paused for a moment, holding up a finger as she lifted a cup of tea to her lips. "My apologies."

"No, it's fine," Denzel replied. "What happened to Ammon? Is he still part of the team here?"

She shook her head. "No, he was dismissed after ..." she hesitated, then sighed. "He became a bit obsessed."

"Obsessed with what?"

She let out a breath. "He became a member of a cult. A small group, but they have a growing presence in the region. They believe that the tomb of Credne is a ... well, a gateway, of sorts. A path to the Otherworld. They believe that if they can gain access to this gateway, they can travel to the world of the gods."

"Heaven?" Denzel asked, his tone skeptical.

She gave a tight smile and a shake of her head. "Not entirely. Not precisely an afterlife. Think of it more like another plane of existence. Another reality, perhaps. Or a parallel world."

Denzel shook his head, his expression strained.

"I know how it sounds," she replied. "Which is exactly why Dr. Warren eventually dismissed Ammon. We felt badly for him if I'm honest. We believed he might be mentally ill. But he truly believes. He talked of it constantly."

"What did he say?" Denzel asked. He was making notes and had written Ammons name, circling it and adding a large question mark. His name was nowhere on the list that Maalyck had given him.

"He had a theory," Tennant said. "He believed that the comparative mythologies of cultures worldwide had their roots in a single, powerful culture. A pre-culture, if you will, dating from a time before any recorded history. Well before even the Phoenicians and Mesopotamians. A culture so old that it is lost to history. It isn't a new theory. There are many in the academic and scientific community who speculate on this. But Ammon believed it deeply. And passionately. He would debate upon it for hours, which became wearying."

"Did Ammon ever do anything beyond talking about this? Any sort of violence? Criminal activity?"

She thought for a moment. "He came into conflict with Dr. Warren and some of the others after taking one of the artifacts. For months, things had gone missing around the site. Equipment, books, some of the molds and models of artifacts kept offsite."

"Molds and models ... " Denzel said. "Did those include any models of the sword? The one Kotler and Maalyck recovered from the brass hall?"

She nodded. "Among other items, yes."

Denzel made a note of this. "Was this why Ammond was fired?"

"Ultimately, I believe so. It was not long after this that Dr. Warren left the site himself. The region came into conflict. The Uprising," she said. "The entire site was shuttered. Dr. Warren continued to lobby for reopening the site, to bring back his team. Dr. Maalyck became more prominent in Egypt's ministry of antiquities, during that time. He was favored because of his heritage and his hard work. I believe he and Dr. Warren eventually came into conflict. Dr. Maalyck wanted Dr. Kotler to be recognized for his role in discovering Credne's hall, and he was pushing for Dr. Kotler to be the lead on site. Dr. Warren was ... less than appreciative."

Denzel made another note. "I think that catches us up to now," he said. "I really appreciate your help, Dr. Tennant."

She smiled and nodded. "Please, do let me know when Dr. Kotler has been found."

They said their goodbyes, and Denzel closed the laptop. He spent another moment jotting things into his notepad, then stood and made his way out into the camp, asking around until he located Maalyck.

"Dr. Ammon Cairo ELsayed," Denzel read from his notes. He looked up. "He's not on your list."

Maalyck shook his head. "No, and perhaps that is an oversight. It's just that I have not seen or thought of him for some time. He left the camp in disgrace, many years ago. I have not spoken to him in several years."

"He knew about the sword? And the chamber?"

Maalyck nodded. "Yes, he was assisting Dr. Warren with the exploration of the chamber, when I joined the team."

"Did you know about his obsession with the Otherworld?"

Maalyck considered for a moment, then shook his head. "Not precisely. I knew that he had become involved in something unseemly. He had joined a local cult, I believe. It has become popular in this region, from what I understand. I also learned that he'd stolen many resources from the camp. I assumed he was dismissed for this."

"And you knew he had a grudge against you?"

Maalyck sighed. "I suppose he must have, though he never confronted me directly. I apologize, Agent Denzel. It never even occurred to me to add his name to the list. I had assumed he was long gone. Do you believe this man abducted Dr. Kotler?"

"It's a hunch, mostly. But I strongly suspect he did," Denzel said. "Do you know how to find him?"

Maalyck thought about this. "I am uncertain, but perhaps my colleagues at the University can help. I know that he occasionally submits papers for peer review. He must have an address on file."

"Find him," Denzel said. "I think Dr. Kotler's life may depend on it."

He checked his watch. They had only a few hours left. It was already getting dark, and the drop site was deep within the mountains.

"What about the sword?" Denzel asked.

Maalyck looked pained. "I have it," he said. "And I have removed the pommel, as you asked. I am ... concerned about this."

Denzel knew exactly why he was so concerned. They were walking a line that might lead to more than just a bit of trouble for the both of them. This was about more than career concerns —they were risking imprisonment, and maybe worse.

It wasn't just Kotler's life on the line now.

"Make your calls and find out what you can about Ammon. And then we need to get you and that sword to the drop point." Denzel paused for a moment. "For Kotler," he said.

Maalyck studied him and nodded.

Denzel left Maalyck to it, wandering back to Kotler's tent.

The tension was building. Everything was stacked against them, at the moment, and anything could cause it all to topple. What made it far worse, however, was the fact that there was very little Denzel could do. This was a waiting game. Not really his strong suit, but he'd manage.

He stepped into the tent and stopped short.

Medo Sarraf, the Ra'id, stood in front of the table Denzel had been using as a desk. The laptop stood open. Denzel knew he'd closed it before leaving. It was password locked, so he wasn't too worried. But Sarraf was blatantly flipping through the notes and scribbles that Denzel had left behind.

"Can I help you, Ra'id?" Denzel asked cautiously.

Sarraf looked up, his expression almost smug, but the threat came through loud and clear.

From outside the tent, two of Sarraf's men entered, standing on either side of Denzel.

"Agent Denzel of the U.S. FBI," Sarraf said. "You are under arrest."

CHAPTER THIRTEEN

FBI Headquarters, Manhattan

LUDLUM LEFT the offices of the video forensics team, feeling frustrated and a little irritated by the lack of progress. They were working every angle, but there was little to find.

Or rather, there was a veritable deluge of things to find—a cascade of infractions and suspicious behavior that triggered red flags at nearly any given moment. There just was no way to filter all that noise and narrow it down to something relevant.

One thing was evident, though: The security force at the site was corrupt.

Ludlum had lost count of the number of clandestine meetings, subtle and not-so-subtle hand-offs of bribes, unidentified strangers allowed access to one or the other of the various mountain chambers at the site, all as the security personnel took casual strolls into the darkness.

Any one of these encounters could have something to do with Kotler's abduction. Or nothing at all. Short of actually spotting Kotler on one of the videos, there was just no way to narrow it all down.

She didn't look forward to updating Denzel on any of this.

It wasn't that she was afraid he'd be angry or that he'd blame her somehow. Rather, she dreaded the report because it wasn't much of a report at all.

At the moment she was living in a sort of Schrödinger's box of hope—as long as she didn't have confirmation that Kotler was dead, then he was still alive. Every report that led nowhere was just one more creak of the lid for that box, and she was afraid that it might fly open at any second and reveal an ugly truth she wasn't prepared to accept.

She returned to her own lab, intent on sucking it up and making the video call. This was the job. And like it or not, dread it or not, right now Denzel needed any scrap of information he could get.

She brought up the app and rang Denzel. It continued for several minutes, with no answer.

She checked her schedule. This was the time they had agreed upon. It wasn't like Denzel to miss a call.

She continued trying for a few more minutes, and only gave up after seeing an email notification slide in at the top right of her screen. It faded before she could catch all the details, but she'd seen the name "Kotler" in the subject line. She switched windows and found the email at the top of her inbox.

It was from Dr. Maalyck, and it wasn't good news.

It wasn't very long, and she read through it twice to make sure she had the details right.

Denzel had given Maalyck her contact information, Maalyck said. Kotler was still missing. Agent Denzel had been arrested. And now Maalyck was unsure what to do.

Maalyck included his username in his email, asking her to

call him as soon as possible, and she immediately rang him from the app.

He answered almost instantly.

"Dr. Ludlum. Thank you for calling me." His voice was strained, and she could see how worried and concerned he was.

"What happened?" Ludlum asked. "You said that Agent Denzel was arrested?"

"Perhaps an hour ago. I contacted you as soon as I learned of this. I have attempted to reach Ra'id Sarraf but have had no success. His subordinates will not tell me where he has gone."

"Did they say why he was arrested?"

Maalyck shook his head. "They hesitated even to confirm his arrest." He looked around him, conspiratorially. "Dr. Ludlum, the deadline to deliver the sword is approaching. I was uncomfortable with this plan even with Agent Denzel was present, but now ..."

He hesitated, and Ludlum nodded. "I understand." She thought for a moment. "Do you have a satellite phone? Aside from the system you're using for internet access?"

Maalyck nodded. "Yes. I have one provided by the museum."

She was thinking. She knew Denzel's general plan, which wasn't that complicated. Maalyck would take the sword to the drop point, Denzel would somehow track the pickup and follow whoever took it. If Kotler wasn't released at the drop point, Denzel would rescue him wherever he was being held. He would also retrieve the sword and arrest whoever was responsible.

It was just the sort of plan Denzel liked. Simple. Straight-forward. But it was also high-risk. There was no way to know how many people were involved in this, and how well armed they might be. And unlike most of the operations Denzel ran, he didn't have the full backup and support of his team at the

FBI. It was just him, from what Ludlum could gather. He certainly couldn't depend on the security force there.

Denzel was taking a huge gamble, not just with Kotler's life but with his own, and with Maalyck's. But Ludlum knew that if there were any other way, Denzel would take it.

Ludlum couldn't replicate Denzel's plan remotely, of course. She'd have to come up with something new and on the fly. And her resources were even more limited, with Denzel out of play.

She'd worry about Denzel later. If he were under arrest, they would take him somewhere to be processed. There would be government paperwork and bureaucracy to wade through. She would alert Agent Brown to all of this, and let the lawyers and diplomats handle it.

Kotler and Maalyck were in more immediate danger.

"Take that satellite phone with you. Can you hide it in whatever you're using to carry the sword?"

Maalyck nodded. "The sword is in a canvas bag. There are several pockets."

"Wrap the phone in something," Ludlum said. "Some socks or underwear maybe. Something to pad it, so that no one feels anything hard if they pat the bag."

"I can do this," Maalyck said. "But you are asking me to continue on with the plan."

"I am," Ludlum said. She hesitated, then played the only card she had. "For Kotler's sake."

Maalyck stared back at her from the screen, then sighed. "Yes," he said. "For Dr. Kotler. It is a great risk for me. Please forgive my hesitation."

Ludlum shook her head. "Not at all! We're going to figure a way to mitigate that risk as much as possible. Do you know the area they've chosen for the drop point?"

"It is deep in the mountains, but I know the place. I explored it often, as a boy. By road, it takes a great deal of time."

"What about by foot?" Ludlum asked.

Maalyck smiled, shaking his head. "I am not in the physical shape of my boyhood, but I could be there in half the time."

"That might not be a bad plan," Ludlum said, thinking. "Are there places to hide, in that area? Someplace you could retreat to quickly?"

"Many places," Maalyck nodded. "I believe I see what you're asking. I can make the drop-off and retreat quickly into the hills. Ammon will expect me to use the roads, which he may have blocked."

Ludlum shook her head. "I'm sorry, who is Ammon?"

Maalyck made a face, as if only realizing that he'd left information out. "I apologize! I was so concerned for Agent Denzel and Dr. Kotler, I neglected to tell you. Dr. Ammon Cairo ELsayed. He is a former assistant of Dr. Warner's but was expelled from the team for stealing artifacts and equipment. Agent Denzel believed he might be the one responsible for Dr. Kotler's abduction. It is unfair of me to assume he is guilty, but I am afraid I am a bit biased."

"Do you have any other information about him? Photos?"

"I can forward you his files," Maalyck said. He began tapping at the laptop on his side, and seconds later Ludlum saw the email notification.

"I'll take a look. For now ... I hate to put you in this position ..."

Maalyck shook his head. "It is not you who put me in this position, Dr. Ludlum. It was Ammon. Or whoever abducted Dr. Kotler."

"What will you do?" Ludlum asked.

"What I must," Dr. Maalyck replied.

She nodded. "Send me the number for that satellite phone. I can put a trace on it from here. It might help."

"I will do this," Maalyck nodded.

Ludlum was about to disconnect but hesitated. "Dr. Maalyck ..." she said. "Please be careful."

Maalyck nodded, and the call ended.

Ludlum sat back, considering everything.

This was trouble. All of it. She knew some lines were being crossed here, but she was rolling with Denzel's plan. More or less.

He wasn't one to break rules for no good reason. But it was possible that he had a blind spot when it came to Dan Kotler.

She could relate.

She checked the time. Dr. Maalyck would have to leave around now if he was to make the rendezvous.

She typed up everything she'd just learned, and included the information about Dr. ELsayed, forwarding everything to the video forensics team. It might help in the search. She knew they were applying facial recognition to the videos as they scrubbed through them, and though most of the faces they found were not in any official databases, they could quickly compare Ammon's photo to the collection they were building.

She hoped it helped.

Now she had another task that wasn't going to be pleasant. She forwarded the files once more, jotting a quick note in the email, then rose from her desk and went to see Agent Brown. She didn't have time to wait for an invitation. They needed to get the gears moving for Agent Denzel.

Wherever Kotler was, she prayed he was ok. But she was also praying for Denzel, for Maalyck, even for herself at this point.

There was more than enough trouble to go around.

CHAPTER FOURTEEN

Egypt

KOTLER STUMBLED UP A SLOPE, his legs feeling rubbery and his neck and back aching. The chains weighed him down like an anchor, and each step was a trial of will. He kept moving, even as his head and body protested, crying for him to fall where he was and just sleep.

He wasn't confident he'd survive if he did that. The cold was already biting, slowing his movements and adding to the pull of exhaustion. If he gave in, he might die of hypothermia here.

There were also other dangers.

There were predatory animals in the region, including a variety of large cats that prowled these hilltops, looking for the sort of prey that might be stumbling around in exhaustion.

Though more dangerous, in Kotler's estimate, were the snakes and scorpions.

He had already spotted and avoided several as he lumbered through the terrain. It didn't help much that he knew there were around thirty species of snakes in Egypt, and half of them were poisonous.

Perhaps he'd been hasty in his assessment of leaving versus staying in the cave.

He was all in at the moment, however. No turning back. His only consolation was that the night was cold, driving snakes and scorpions alike to burrow deeper into any place where they could conserve warmth. This left the more obvious paths clear, and a bit safer. Now he had only to worry about predators dropping on him from above or slipping and finding himself spiraling down the rocky cliff face.

So that was something.

It would help immensely if he could rid himself of the chains.

The cuffs around his wrists were thick iron. It might be possible to damage them enough to remove them, but it would take hours, and he lacked the leverage to do it properly. The links of the chain, however, were more vulnerable.

He stopped, looking around to see if he could spot anything useful. There were several toppled stones, much like the one he'd used back in the cave. They would have to do.

He found a boulder that had a nice rounded peak. He prodded around the base of it with the iron rod, making sure none of the aforementioned snakes were hiding there. He then performed this same check on the pile of stones he planned to pilfer. A scorpion, alarmed by his prodding, rushed out of a gap in the rocks, and Kotler let it pass, unmolested.

He nudged the stones a bit more and finally chose one that had a bit of a wedge shape, almost like an axe head. He hoped this might give him some advantage.

Back at the boulder, he considered his options. His energy was waning, and so he needed to do this as efficiently as possible. After mulling it over for a long while, he decided the best approach was to focus all of his energy on the center link, where the chain that connected the foot shackles linked to the chain that stretched between his wrists.

It wasn't ideal from a leverage standpoint. He could only get so much range of motion before pulling the chain off of the boulder. It meant working in a tight arc and relying more on muscle than gravity to help with the work. That cost him.

It was exhausting and painful, piling on to Kotler's physical and emotional misery, and he stopped several times, crying and yelling in frustration. Not his finest moment, by his own estimate.

The events of the past few days were taking their toll.

He channeled his frustration into the work, slamming the edge of the stone down with a building rage.

His hands felt achy and raw, and every muscle burned from his wrists to his lower back. His vision was starting to blur and darken, though he wasn't sure if that was from the exertion or if it might not be the deep Egyptian night.

He couldn't keep this up. He could already feel himself drooping, giving in to the exhaustion.

He shook himself. Blinked. Huffed a few times, getting oxygen and blood flowing. And then he gripped the stone and struck as hard as he could.

The link severed.

It was a small gap, but seeing it nearly made Kotler weep with relief.

He got to his feet, standing wobblily, and shook himself. He looped the chain around the boulder, pulling and trying to widen the gap he'd just created.

It was useless. His arms were too weak, and no matter how he pulled the link wouldn't bend. The gap, as promising as it had seemed, wasn't enough.

He needed more leverage.

He looked around, hoping for any inspiration. His resources were as limited as his reserves of strength. But maybe ... maybe ...

His eyes landed on the wedge of stone, and he had an idea.

Once again, he took up the iron rod and prodded the pile of stones. No scorpions this time. He took up the biggest stone he could lift, an oblong globe of rock that resembled an enormous potato. It should be heavy enough to do the trick. He hoped.

The next steps were tricky. He knelt to the ground, finding a soft patch of soil. Through a bit of wrangling, he managed to wedge the edge of the original stone into the gap in the link. It wasn't much, and he ultimately had to drive the rod into the soil and lean the wedged stone against it, to keep the whole thing upright. It was a start. He now hefted the heavier rock, balancing it on the broader portion of the wedge, and then leaned into it.

He bounced, using his weight for momentum, and praying that the combination of his body and the stone would create the pressure he needed. It would have been more effective to lift the stone and slam it down, but he lacked both the leverage and the strength.

After several minutes he set the stones aside and inspected the link.

And grinned.

The gap had widened significantly. Not yet enough to allow another link to pass through, but close. This plan was working, at least.

He set up the process again, repeating his steps. When he next checked his progress, he didn't even have to try to pull the chains free. The link connecting the foot shackles fell free as he was lifting the chain from the ground. Kotler unhooked the broken link then, and stood, his hands finally free to drop to his sides. Each still had a short length of chain dangling, but on the whole, it was less cumbersome than it had been.

He was elated by the victory. He still felt cold, hungry, exhausted. His body still ached, and he wasn't even sure he had the energy to move another step. But he felt freer than he had for hours.

He bent to pull the iron rod out of the ground and felt suddenly light-headed.

He went to his knees, and braced himself against the boulder, trying to let the feeling pass. All he had to do was keep it together, to keep going. He could find help soon. He was free.

He'd worked so hard, and he was free.

It was the last thought he had before collapsing into unconsciousness.

CHAPTER FIFTEEN

FBI Headquarters, Manhattan

Agent Brown stood and was leaning against the frame of the office window, watching Ludlum as the details were laid out. Ludlum told her about Denzel's arrest, and about Ammon. She left out the details about Denzel's plan and Maalyck's part in it. She wasn't sure how much Brown knew about the exchange, and had the feeling that Denzel was keeping it on the down low.

Ludlum was also standing, hands on the back of the chair in front of Denzel's desk and her back to the closed door of the office. When she was done giving her report, Brown shook her head and cursed.

"This just got a lot worse," she said.

Ludlum nodded. "What do we do?"

Brown shook her head. "Officially, the US has no presence on that site. Agent Denzel is there as a civilian. Unofficially ... well, he's one of ours. I'll make some calls. Someone in the State Department will want to know this is happening."

Ludlum huffed. "At least we have a lead on Dr. Kotler's abduction," she said.

Brown regarded her for a moment and gave a slight shake of her head. Then said, "At least there's that."

Ludlum picked up on the tone and had a sudden flash of irritation. "Agent Brown, do you have some sort of problem with Dr. Kotler?"

Brown chuckled. "A bit, yeah. But only that he always seems to be at the center of everything, when trouble goes down. His professor tries to steal state secrets. His brother is kidnapped. His girlfriend, also kidnapped, during that Viking thing. Not to mention his *other* girlfriend being the head of one of the biggest international smuggling operations in history. And Kotler himself ... he's been abducted so many times, his milk cartons could fill the dairy aisle of a Costco."

Ludlum regarded her for a moment, feeling the frustration and anger welling up. And then she sighed, nodded, and said, "You're right."

Brown's eyes widened. "I am? I thought for sure this was the part where we started yelling at each other. I know you and Kotler are an item."

"Sort of," Ludlum said. "We're ... taking it slow."

Brown laughed. "Taking it slow. I've heard that one before."

"He's had some ... *unique* problems with relationships," Ludlum said.

They both paused for a moment, and then both broke out laughing. It was loud and long and hard, and Ludlum ended up leaning over the chair in front of her, putting her hands over her face. She straightened up and saw that Agent Brown was also rubbing tears from her eyes, still laughing.

"I'm sorry," Ludlum said. "I know you're doing what you're trained to do. Be suspicious. Look for the out of place details."

"That's right," Brown nodded. "That's what I'm trained to do. But Liz, it's not personal, ok? It's just that something bugs me about Kotler, and I'm not sure what it is. And because of that, I have to be cautious. I have to look closer."

Ludlum considered this and nodded. "You're not wrong, you know."

"About which part?" Brown asked.

"It's suspicious. All of it. Dan is a magnet for this kind of thing. And something that NSA agent told us—"

"Agent Coben," Brown said.

Ludlum nodded again. "Right. Coben. He asked the same questions. Why Kotler?"

"More than that," Brown replied. "Why Historic Crimes? How did this division even get a foothold in the Bureau? As far as I know, someone just tapped Agent Denzel on the shoulder and handed him the keys."

Ludlum shrugged. "Is it really that unusual? I'm new to the Bureau, but isn't this kind of like a task force? Someone from up top saw a need, and figured Agent Denzel could fill it?"

"It was more like someone thought Dr. Kotler could fill it, and that he could use a resource like the FBI to get things done," Brown said. "And honestly, that bothers the hell out of me."

"Bothers you? Why?"

"Because it hints at something I don't like," Brown replied. "It hints that someone above our pay grade has an agenda involving Kotler and has enough power to put an entire division of the FBI at his disposal."

Ludlum thought about this for a moment.

"But why?"

Brown shook her head. "If I knew that, it wouldn't bug me so much. But right now, we need to get the gears moving on

Agent Denzel's arrest. I'll make some calls. And I'm approving your request to put a trace on that satellite phone."

Ludlum nodded and excused herself, leaving Denzel's office and making her way downstairs. She was headed to her lab, more out of habit than out of purpose. But she stopped at the door. She couldn't think of what she'd do, once she was back at her desk.

She'd handed off her caseload to the specialists working under her, and though she knew this was making their work-loads heavy, she didn't think it would be productive to go reclaim any of that work. It would just cause confusion and problems, to hand it off so frequently. She'd interrupt a process in motion, and potentially introduce errors. Plus, she knew she'd inevitably be pulled back into the events tied to Kotler's abduction. It wasn't fair that her team had to carry the brunt of the work, but it would be even more unfair for her to interfere just to dump it on them a second time.

Still, she couldn't sit by and do nothing.

She glanced back at Agent Denzel's office, where Agent Brown was already on the phone to the State Department or whoever else might help them with this mess.

Why Historic Crimes?

It was a fair question. And one Ludlum hadn't really thought much about. But Kotler ...

She wasn't sure how she felt about Kotler. She liked him. She found him attractive, as much for his intelligence as for his looks. She knew he had a reputation for being something of a playboy, but in the past year or so she hadn't seen much evidence of that. If anything, she got the impression that Kotler was still reeling from his past couple of relationships.

It was his idea to take things slow.

Ludlum had no real issue with it. Years of dodging men who just wanted to get into her pants had given her an appreciation for genuine gentlemen. But she also wanted someone to want her. Kotler seemed to, but he hesitated.

She knew it was mostly because of Gail McCarthy.

For nearly two years, Gail had manipulated not only Kotler but the FBI and a number of other law enforcement agencies worldwide. She'd been a master at it, playing everyone in a long game that ultimately resulted in her and Kotler facing off head-to-head. What would that do to someone, to have the person they loved endanger everyone in their life, everyone and everything they cared about? And then to be the one to pull the trigger and end it ...

Ludlum realized she'd been standing with her hand on the door to the forensics lab. She glanced around and saw that one of the agents was watching from his cubicle. He looked as if he were about to stand and move toward her, maybe to ask if she were alright. She smiled at him, shook her head and sighed as if she were just crazy busy, lost in her own head. She waved to him as she opened the door and went into her lab.

Whatever it was between her and Kotler, it was going to take time to see it out. It was going to take him more than a minute to get over Gail McCarthy, of course. And maybe ... well, maybe he would never be ready. Ludlum had to be prepared for that.

But he wouldn't have a chance—*they* wouldn't have a chance—unless he could be found and rescued.

Right now, people were dealing with that, as best they could. People were dealing with getting help for Agent Denzel. People were even dealing with the standard, day-to-day workload of the forensics lab.

But no one was dealing with the question that Agent Brown had asked.

Why Historic Crimes?

It was something Ludlum could do. Something to focus on,

to keep her mind off of the lack of progress, and off of worrying over Kotler and Denzel. It was at least loosely related to the case at hand. And it wasn't pressing, so if she had to step away from it and attend to something else, she could.

Call it a side hobby, Ludlum thought.

She sat down at her desk and opened her laptop.

She paused, her fingers hovering over the keys, just on the verge of typing her password to log into the FBI's intranet.

What if someone doesn't want anyone looking closer?

The question made her uneasy for a moment. And then it made her set her jaw and log in, her fingers striking the keys with purpose.

Looking closer, finding the story in the details, even when those details were scarce, and especially when someone didn't want anyone to notice—that was just about the best way to sum up Ludlum's job description as she could imagine.

She still prayed Kotler and Denzel would be ok. She worried for both of them. Especially Kotler. But she saved a bit of worry for herself.

There was no way to know what sort of hornet's nest she might be kicking.

CHAPTER SIXTEEN

Egypt

DENZEL WAS handcuffed and in the back of a military issue transport truck. It looked for all the world like every other military transport he'd ever been in. His years in the service had involved a lot of hot, bone-jarring rides in trucks like these. At least this time he wasn't loaded down in fatigues and a helmet. Though he wouldn't have objected to having body armor and a weapon in his hands.

The Ra'id still hadn't told him why he was under arrest. He'd had his men load Denzel into the truck and chain him to the floor. The truck's rear door had been shut and locked tight, and soon the engine started, and they were rumbling along. There were no windows and no light. The Egyptian night was clear, and the moon and stars were out, but there was barely a sliver of that light penetrating the truck.

Denzel had to content himself with listening as the truck's gears ground and the engine revved.

Sometime later—Denzel estimated about a little over an

hour—the truck stopped. The engine was shut off, and the vehicle rocked slightly as a door opened and then slammed closed. Denzel heard the sound of feet on gravel.

A moment later, the back door swung open, and Denzel saw a lone figure standing there, faintly illuminated by moonlight, holding a gun.

"Ra'id Sarraf?" Denzel asked, confused.

"Hold your hands out in front of you," the Sarraf ordered.

Denzel did as he was told, and Sarraf climbed into the truck. He stood in front of Denzel and unlocked the chain. "Climb down," he commanded.

Denzel, confused, did as he was told.

Something wasn't right.

Where were Sarraf's men? Why was he the only one here, and where was here, anyway?

"Stand there," Sarraf commanded as Denzel reached the ground. He was pointing to a spot several feet from the truck. Denzel moved toward it, taking in the location as he walked.

The area where they were parked was wide and open—no buildings or other structures. The spot was in a small valley, a bowl formed by the mountains around them. Denzel could see a road stretching into the night, presumably the direction from which they'd arrived, given the orientation of the truck. He turned to face the opposite direction, his hands cuffed in front of him, and the scene was nearly identical.

They were in the middle of nowhere, for reasons Denzel hadn't been told, with a single, armed man glaring down at him from the back of the military transport.

Denzel might not know what was happening exactly, but he didn't have to. He knew he was in trouble.

Sarraf climbed down from the truck, holding to the door frame with one hand, gripping the rifle with the other. It was an awkward and vulnerable move, but Denzel was far enough away that he could never close the gap and seize Sarraf's weapon. Likewise, the area was so open that there was nowhere to take cover if he decided to run.

This was strategic. And it was bad news.

"Sarraf, what am I doing here? You said I was under arrest. Where are we?"

Sarraf stepped toward him. "We wait," he said.

"Wait?" Denzel asked. "What for ..." he paused, his eyes wide. "You? You're the one who abducted Kotler?"

Sarraf ignored him.

"Is he here?"

Sarraf turned on him, raising his weapon and pointing it directly at Denzel's head.

"The Alihat Iadida have asked me to bring you here, but they did not specify that you must be alive. You will be silent."

Denzel said nothing, and after a moment Sarraf lowered his weapon and took a position beside Denzel.

They waited.

Denzel kept himself busy by calculating his odds of survival, and the numbers didn't look good.

He had no idea where he was, though he did have some general sense of the direction they'd come from. He was unarmed. Sarraf was very armed and was also a trained military officer who likely knew his weapon better then he knew most human beings. And Denzel was handcuffed—not entirely unworkable, but it did provide some limitations.

The chances were pretty good that he'd end this evening by being shot.

They were also pretty good that this had something to do with Kotler's abduction. Which meant it had something to do with that Irish god's tomb.

After several minutes, Denzel spotted the flicker of head-lights in the distance. A few minutes later a jeep pulled in

beside the truck, the lights and engine shutting off simultane-
ously. A man stepped out and walked toward them.

He was Egyptian, as far as Denzel could tell. But not military. He was tall, and a bit thin. He wore everyday street
clothes—jeans and an untucked button-up shirt, the sleeves
rolled slightly. He wore glasses and had a neatly cropped beard.

"What is he doing here?" the man asked, his voice cracking
slightly. He motioned to Denzel with a thin, shaking hand.

"He was causing trouble," Sarraf replied. "The Alihat
Iadida requested that I bring him. We can take care of all of
them together. Where is the doctor?"

"At the cave," the man replied.

The doctor, Denzel thought. *Kotler.* And he didn't like the
sound of *we can take care of all of them together.*

"What about Maalyck?" the man asked. "Do you know if
he will do it?"

Sarraf made a noise. "He is already on his way. My men
reported that he left shortly after I did."

The man nodded and fidgeted.

Denzel knew who he was now. It was his question about
Maalyck that was the tell. This was Dr. Ammon ELsayed—the
man who had been booted from the camp by Dr. Warren, for
stealing equipment and artifacts. He was a member of a cult,
Dr. Tennant had said.

What was it that Sarraf kept saying? *Alibaba Iota?* Something like that. It had to be the name of the cult.

Sarraf was a part of it, too.

This was looking worse by the minute.

They waited in the dark, and Ammon kept checking his
watch. "It is nearly time. I do not see his truck. He should be
here."

"He will be here," Sarraf said, though he sounded tense,
even a little angry.

Just then there was a sound from off to the side, and all three men turned to see what it was.

A figure, obscured by the darkness, suddenly rushed into a gap in the hillside, escaping into the mountains.

"Halt!" Sarraf shouted, taking aim. He fired a few rounds into the hills, and the noise echoed through the little canyon and into the night.

"It must be Maalyck!" Ammon shouted.

Denzel made his move.

He leapt, raising his hands and looping them over Sarraf's head. He pulled back, letting the handcuffs dig into the man's neck.

Sarraf struggled, dropping his rifle and clutching at his throat, at Denzel's hands, even reaching back to try to gouge Denzel's eyes.

Denzel easily avoided the man's clumsy attempts and kept the pressure on. He was putting pressure on Sarraf's carotid artery. The man should black out soon.

Suddenly a series of shots rang out again, and Denzel, startled, looked up to see Ammon, holding Sarraf's weapon and aiming it into the air. He brought the barrel down and pointed at Denzel's head. "Let him go!" Ammon shouted. "Now!"

Denzel eased up on Sarraf, and slowly raised his hands back over the Ra'id's head.

Sarraf coughed and rubbed his throat but took a pistol from a holster on his hip and used it to slam into Denzel's temple.

Denzel went to his knees, dazed but holding to consciousness. He blinked, seeing flashes of light in his vision.

"Stay down!" Sarraf shouted, pressing the pistol to Denzel's head.

Denzel intended to do exactly that. He had no cards to play here. He'd taken his shot and failed. Now, it was anyone's game.

"Watch him!" Sarraf said to Ammon and then ran into the gap in the hillside, chasing Maalyck.

Ammon had stepped back and was holding the rifle on Denzel, breathing heavily as if he'd just run here from a great distance. The barrel of the gun wobbled slightly as Ammon gripped it, but he was so close there was no chance he'd miss if he pulled the trigger.

Denzel kept very still. He was on his knees, hands cuffed in front of him, head looking anywhere but at Ammon. No eye contact. The man was nervous, and that might make him trigger happy. Denzel would play it cool for now. He was a kneeling statue.

Several minutes later Sarraf returned, shoving an injured Maalyck ahead of him. He had the pistol pressed into Maalyck's back and was carrying a duffel bag in his free hand.

He shoved Maalyck as they approached. "On your knees," he said.

Maalyck did as he was told, kneeling beside Denzel. "Hands on your head," Sarraf said, and Maalyck obeyed.

The Ra'id took out another pair of handcuffs, and as he handed the duffel back to Ammon, he cuffed Maalyck.

Ammon unzipped the bag and took out an objected wrapped in cloth. He carefully unwrapped it, then held it up to catch the light.

The bronze sword.

Ammon dropped the bag to the ground, and held the sword out, admiring it in the moonlight.

"We have done it," Ammon whispered.

"Now we go to the cave," Sarraf said.

"Yes," Ammon nodded, still studying the sword with an air of reverence.

"Help me load them," Sarraf said, pulling at each of the men on the ground and forcing them ahead, toward the truck.

Ammon held his weapon on them, ready to shoot if they made any move he didn't like. To Denzel's relief, the man seemed calmer than before. He'd gotten his prize, plus he'd put his enemy in his place. He seemed almost smug about it.

Whatever kept him from shooting was fine by Denzel. For now.

Maalyck had to have some help getting into the truck. He'd taken a bullet in his upper left leg. It wasn't bad, from what Denzel could see. It had punched through the meaty part of his leg, on the side, missing the bone entirely. He would be alright, but he'd need medical attention soon.

Sarraf locked both of them into the truck, seating them facing each other. "Throw the bag in here," he said to Ammon. "We will leave no trace."

Ammon tossed the bag up into the truck, and then Sarraf hopped down and closed the door. Denzel heard it lock.

Moments later he heard the smaller truck start, followed by the crunch of gravel. The transport's engine roared to life again then, and they rumbled away.

"Just stay calm," he said to Maalyck. "We're going to figure a way out of this."

"We may already have a way," Maalyck said, gritting his teeth. He nodded to the bag. "Your Dr. Ludlum advised me to put a satellite phone in that bag."

Denzel's eyes went wide, and then he grinned. "I'm going to have to give that woman a raise."

He stood then, as best he could. Neither he nor Maalyck was close enough to reach the bag with their hands, but Denzel was able to lay on the floor and hook the bag with his feet. He dragged it to him and then rifled through it until he found the phone, wrapped in several undershirts.

He took one of the shirts out and tossed it to Maalyck. "Tie that around your leg, a couple of inches above the wound. Make it tight."

Maalyck did as he was told, with Denzel giving a few more instructions and finally nodding. He then turned his attention to the satellite phone.

He punched in a number and was about to make the call when the truck slowed, and finally came to a stop.

He quickly kicked the bag toward Maalyck. "Tell them you took the shirt out of there, to use as a tourniquet."

Maalyck nodded, and Denzel shoved the phone into the front pocket of his jeans. Sarraf had searched him when he was arrested, so Denzel hoped he wouldn't think to do it again. It was a gamble, but they were at a point where the risks of not taking chances outweighed the dangers of discovery.

They sat in silence in the truck, waiting. After a long moment, however, there was a sound from outside. One Denzel hadn't expected.

It was a cry of rage and frustration

Denzel smiled and laughed lightly, and Maalyck gave him a strange look.

"It's Kotler," Denzel whispered. "He's escaped."

CHAPTER SEVENTEEN

KOTLER WOKE to a splitting headache and a tickle on his arm.

It was still dark, but the moon was out and giving him at least some light. With some effort he turned his head slightly, feeling the grit of dirt and pebbles under his cheek, and looked at his arm. And froze.

A scorpion—maybe the same one he'd rousted from its home earlier—had crawled onto his arm and was perched, as if staring at him. *Your move*, it seemed to say.

Kotler breathed slowly, unmoving. It was likely the thing was just looking for warmth, and Kotler was a decent source of it. If he hadn't awoken when he had, it might have eventually found its way into Kotler's clothing, maybe nestling into his armpit. Or ... other areas.

There were no comfortable directions for this line of thought, and Kotler pulled his mind back, focusing on the problem literally facing him.

A sting, now, would be disastrous. Kotler had to figure a way to get this creature off of him without startling it.

Kotler had collapsed face-down on the ground, his hands

extended in front of him. The iron cuffs on his wrists, along with the short lengths of chain still attached to them, weighed his arms down. Which may have been the only thing that had saved him from a sting already, now that he thought about it. He hadn't moved his arms when he awoke.

It also meant any movement he made now would be slower. A quick flick of the wrist or brush of the fingers might have been enough to send the scorpion on its way, but it was practically impossible to make such a precision move in Kotler's current state. The weight of his arms was one factor. He was also exhausted; his physical strength had been spent on severing the chain. And now the remaining shackles added to the challenge of dealing with this threat.

But maybe the also gave him an advantage.

With concentrated effort, Kotler slowly lifted his left arm, letting the chain dangle and drag in the dirt. It took a lot of energy that Kotler could hardly spare, but he cautiously moved his arm closer to the scorpion.

It reacted by turning, opening and flexing its pincers, and curling its tail for a strike against this new threat.

Kotler eyed the stinger, and despite the creepy-crawling feeling of the scorpion's legs on his arm, he kept his movements slow and deliberate. His arm was shaking from the effort, but that only helped, making the chain undulate slightly and keeping the scorpion's attention fixed on it.

Eventually, the chain swayed within an inch of the arachnid. The scorpion reacted then, striking with its tail.

Kotler used that distraction to his advantage, bringing his left hand down so that the iron shackle brushed the scorpion off of his arm.

He moved his right arm quickly and rolled onto his left side, away from but facing the creature.

The scorpion danced, moving backward and to the side, claws and tail raised in warning. It was mad, but it was leaving.

Kotler watched it go, and then scrambled to his feet, swaying slightly but able to move away from the spot.

He saw the iron rod on the ground, near where he'd fallen earlier. He carefully bent to retrieve it, conscious of his breathing, and picked the rod up.

It felt as if it weighed a hundred pounds, but Kotler knew that was the physical exhaustion talking. The rod was just about the only weapon he had, at the moment, and he wasn't ready to give it up. He wedged it into his belt, like a sword, and then hobbled away from the spot. He left the chains and ankle shackles among the rocks, glad to be rid of them.

While his movement was less encumbered now, the cost had been more of his personal energy than he could spare. He needed rest. He needed food and water.

The cold had crept back upon him, once he'd collapsed and no longer had the warmth of exertion from trying to break the chains. He held his arms close to his chest and hunched as he walked, trying to warm his core.

Everything ached. Everything screamed.

If he didn't find help soon, he was going to die out here.

He stumbled on for an indeterminate amount of time but stopped suddenly as he heard the sound of an engine approaching from the distance.

Down below, veiled by the darkness, a road slowly appeared, illuminated by the headlights of an approaching vehicle.

Kotler recognized it immediately. It was the same vehicle that had delivered him to the cave.

Ammon.

Kotler took cover, though he knew rationally that no one could possibly spot him here, hiding in the hills. He watched as the truck entered into a larger gap in the mountains, pulling in beside a much bigger vehicle. In the headlights, Kotler spotted two men standing, watching the approach. He recognized them instantly.

It was the Ra'id, Medo Sarraf, the head of military security at the Credne site. He was holding a rifle in one hand and had the other clasped on the arm of another man.

Roland Denzel.

Kotler felt a sick dread creep over him. Denzel was clearly a prisoner. His hands appeared to be cuffed in front of him, and even from this distance, Kotler could see the agent's body language. He was playing cautious, and apparently had no plan for an escape. Denzel was biding his time, looking for an opening. But he could use backup.

Kotler knew he was in no shape to take anyone on, much less an armed and trained military man like Sarraf. Despite this, he edged closer, making his way down among the larger rocks, keeping cover as he went.

He could hear their voices, echoing among the hills.

"What is he doing here?" Ammon asked as he approached Sarraf and Denzel.

"He was causing trouble," Sarraf replied. "The Alihat Iadida requested that I bring him. We can take care of all of them together. Where is the doctor?"

Kotler knew they meant him, but he was suddenly caught up by something else they'd said.

Sarraf had used the phrase *Alihat Iadida*.

Kotler recognized it, if only for the language. It was Arabic, for *new gods*.

The New Gods requested that I bring him.

The cult, Kotler realized. The group Ammon had fallen in with, and the reason he'd made a replica of the sword. The

Alihat Iadida were looking for a path to the Otherworld and were manipulating people and events to find it.

And the Ra'id, Sarraf, was a member of their organization.

It explained a lot, including how Ammon had been booted from the project for stealing but had not been arrested by the Egyptian government. He'd had an inside man. And likely more than one.

Who were the Alihat Iadida? Their name hinted at something that tickled Kotler's exhausted mind, but he couldn't quite click to it. He needed to focus, for his sake and for Denzel's.

There was suddenly a shout from below, followed by weapons fire. Kotler ducked, worried that perhaps he'd been spotted. But as he peered over the stone in front of him, he saw Denzel practically garrote Sarraf with his handcuffs, choking the man from behind.

There was a brief flash of hope from Kotler, until he saw Ammon pick up Sarraf's rifle and fire shots into the air.

Denzel released Sarraf, who immediately drew a pistol and slammed it into Denzel's head, sending the agent to his knees. Kotler held his breath as Sarraf pressed the barrel of the gun against Denzel's head, and let it out in relief as Sarraf barked an order to Ammon and went running into a gap in the hills.

A short time later, Sarraf emerged with another man in tow.

Martook Maalyck.

Maalyck was limping and seemed to have injured his leg. He was thrust forward and commanded to get to his knees.

Sarraf handed a duffel bag to Ammon then, and Ammon opened it to take out a cloth-wrapped bundle. He unwound the cloth, and in the glint of moonlight Kotler watched as Ammon tossed the bag aside and held up the bronze sword as if he'd just freed it from a stone.

Kotler could also see that the sword was missing its jeweled pommel.

A small victory, but he would take anything he could get right now.

As Kotler lay against the large rocks, he felt helpless to do anything. He watched as Denzel and Maalyck were loaded into the truck, and then both vehicles moved away, their headlights dancing on the cliff faces as they passed deeper into the mountains.

They were going back to the cave, Kotler knew. Back to where Ammon expected to find Kotler, chained and waiting.

There was no way to know what they would do to Denzel and Maalyck, once they discovered that Kotler was gone.

Kotler tried not to think about it. Instead, he turned his attention to the path Maalyck had used to get to the drop point.

Maalyck had arrived on foot. Maybe he had a vehicle parked back that way, somewhere in the mountains. If Kotler could find it, he could use it to drive out and get help.

Kotler carefully picked his way down the mountainside. He found the opening that Maalyck had used and walked into it, stopping frequently and leaning against the rock face for support. The stone of the mountain rose to either side of him, and this tiny gorge formed a sort of walled path that twisted along, relatively easy to navigate, though it occasionally blocked the moonlight, throwing Kotler into complete darkness.

Kotler pushed through his exhaustion, the ache of his body, the dehydration and hunger. He kept moving, one heavy step after another, stopping for a quick rest if he needed it, but always pressing forward.

Until suddenly the narrow path opened up, and he could see a sort of valley of tents and lights and small trailers below.

The Credne dig site.

Kotler nearly wept with relief, but conserved his energy,

using it to drive one foot in front of the other more quickly now. He fell, picked himself up, and kept moving until, finally, he stumbled into the camp.

He was noticed almost immediately, and a gaggle of archaeologists and researchers rushed forward, called for help, and guided Kotler to one of the tents.

As he lay there, under the ministrations of a medic, he was given water and soup, medications and medical treatments.

They asked him questions, which he was incapable of answering at the moment. He tried to tell them about Denzel, about Maalyck, about Sarraf and Ammon. His words were an indecipherable mumble.

Eventually, he dropped out of consciousness altogether, his body demanding rest. Even as he slipped into a deep sleep, however, one thought stayed firm in his mind.

Denzel was still out there. And he needed Kotler's help.

CHAPTER EIGHTEEN

FBI Headquarters, Manhattan

"We have a problem," Agent Brown said as she barged through Ludlum's door.

Ludlum had been reading up on the department's operating charter, looking for any hints or details about the establishment of Historic Crimes. In particular, she'd been looking for any indication of who had created the charter in the first place. So far, she'd had very little luck.

Her first thought, when Brown entered so abruptly, was that it had something to do with this research. Ludlum found herself clicking away from the charter document as if she'd been caught looking at pornography.

"Denzel is not under arrest by the Egyptian government," Brown stated.

Ludlum blinked. "What? What do you mean?"

Brown shook her head. "No record of his arrest. No order for it. There's a record that he entered the country. He actually cleared his trip with Egyptian officials, just in case they had an objection to an FBI agent visiting in an unofficial capacity." She shook her head. "I don't even think I'd have done that."

Ludlum stared for a moment, slack-jawed. "I don't ... Dr. Maalyck told me that Denzel had been arrested."

"We're having trouble reaching Maalyck, to get more details," Brown replied. "I'm taking a little heat from the State Department. Are you sure Maalyck didn't get this wrong?"

Ludlum hesitated, then shook her head. "I have no idea. I passed along everything he gave me."

"Well, there's nothing on the official record. I'm still trying to get in touch with the head of security there. Medo Sarraf. He's Egyptian military. If Denzel was taken into custody, Sarraf would have given the order."

"Are his people saying anything?" Ludlum asked.

Brown shook her head. "Silent as a tomb right now. They're under orders not to speak to me directly, which puts me in oven mitts at this piano. So going through official channels is going to be a little slow. I'm hoping to reach someone in the camp who can talk to me and give me the scoop. Do you have any other contacts there?"

Ludlum thought for a moment. "No, I was only in contact with Denzel and Maalyck. But I can help. I'll reach out and see who I can connect with."

"That would help," Brown nodded.

"What about the trace?" Ludlum asked.

"It was approved, but I haven't gotten to looking at the report yet."

Ludlum hesitated. "We need to look at that. It could tell us where Maalyck is."

Brown considered this. "What haven't you told me?" she asked.

Ludlum sighed and started explaining Denzel's plan, for Maalyck to deliver the sword so that Denzel could track whoever was behind all of this. "After Agent Denzel was arrested, I told Maalyck to plant the phone in the bag, so we could trace it."

Brown shook her head. "That was good thinking, but ... I can think of at least a dozen reasons why this was a bad call all around." She studied Ludlum. "Denzel put this together?"

"I don't know his reasoning, but yes."

"And you went along with it," Brown said.

"Yes," Ludlum replied.

Brown paused, then blew out a breath. "I wish you'd told me, Liz."

"Where does this put us?" Ludlum asked. She wasn't sure if she meant only as far as the case went, or something more consequential.

Brown sighed and shrugged. "It puts us with a lead we can explore, which is more than we had five minutes ago. I'll check in on this, see what we can learn."

Ludlum nodded.

"There could be some trouble from this," Brown said, eyeing her.

"I know," Ludlum said. "I'll deal with whatever consequences come my way."

Brown shook her head. "No, I mean there could be trouble for Denzel. Maybe a little for you, but ... this was his plan. I'm surprised. He knows protocol. He usually sticks to the rules." She thought for a moment. "Except ... when Kotler's involved."

Ludlum felt herself getting angry but took a calming breath. "He's doing what he believes he has to do," she said tightly. "To make sure Dan is recovered safely."

Brown nodded. "I know that. But this is bigger than Denzel and Kotler. It's bigger than this department. What he's done ..." she huffed, shaking her head. "If it gets out that he asked

Maalyck to steal that sword and hand it over as ransom, it could create an international incident. Not good."

"No," Ludlum agreed. She stood and squared off with Agent Brown. "So it's up to us to make sure this doesn't turn into an incident. We find them. We help them in whatever way we can. And we get everyone back alive."

Brown studied her, then nodded. "I'll do my part. I can't promise we'll be able to skirt any trouble that might fall from this tree, but I'll see what I can do. If you can get us a contact in that camp, do it."

Ludlum nodded, and Brown turned and left the room.

Turning back to her laptop, Ludlum let out a breath she hadn't realized she'd been holding. She dropped into her chair and got to work.

CHAPTER NINETEEN

Egypt

KOTLER AWOKE to someone standing next to his cot.

Dr. Nesahor—the man who had picked them up from town upon their arrival—was bent slightly, looking at Kotler's face.

"I apologize if I woke you," he said quietly.

Kotler tried to speak but found his throat dry, his voice no more than a croak.

Nesahor picked up a water bottle from beside the bed and put a straw to Kotler's lips.

Kotler sipped, and then sputtered a bit. He hadn't realized how thirsty he'd been. He tried to sit up, and Nesahor assisted him.

"You must take things slow," Nesahor said. "You were quite dehydrated. We have two trained medical doctors as part of our team, and they have both examined and treated you. Both say you were close to dying. It is a very stressful thing for the body."

Kotler heard this, and as his brain processed everything in slow motion, he chuckled. Even to him, it sounded like a small, raspy cough. Nesahor patted his back gently, attempting to help.

Kotler shook his head and held up a hand. He was relieved to see they had removed the shackles and bandaged his wounds. His arms felt light, as if he might fling them over his head with just the slightest effort.

"Agent Denzel ..." Kotler started. He cleared his throat and sipped more water. "Denzel and Maalyck ..."

Nesahor shook his head sadly. "Dr. Maalyck is missing. No one knows where he went, and we fear he may have been abducted as well. The security force here has put the camp in lockdown while they investigate."

Kotler shook his head. "He's with Denzel. Sarraf took him. Sarraf and Ammon are working together."

"Ammon?" Nesahor frowned. "Dr. ELsayed?"

"He and Sarraf both belong to ... belong to ..." Kotler struggled, trying to remember.

Arabic. New Gods.

"Alihat Iadida," Kolter rasped as it finally came to him.

Nesahor's eyes widened. "Where did you hear this name?" he asked, glancing around and speaking quietly.

Kotler also looked around. They were in a tent, and other beds were present.

He thought back to the briefing that Maalyck had sent him, the resources and layout of the camp. This was the infirmary—a medical tent. Meant to take care of minor medical issues, but fully stocked in case of an emergency.

Kotler shifted his position, dropping his feet to the floor. Nesahor protested, trying to gently push Kotler back to a prone position, but Kotler shook him off. "I need to make a call. I need to reach my people back in the US. The FBI." He looked up to Nesahor. "Help me get to my tent. Is my laptop still there?"

Nesahor nodded. "Agent Denzel was using your tent as a

base of operations while searching for you. Everything you brought with you is still there."

Kotler stood, a bit shaky, and steadied himself using Nesahor's shoulder. He pulled an IV from his arm and looked down at himself. "Where are my pants?" He was wearing a flimsy hospital gown that ended around mid-thigh.

"We disposed of your clothing," Nesahor replied.

Kotler sighed but nodded. "Get me to my tent."

ONCE BACK AT THE TENT, Kotler paused long enough to pull on clothes. He didn't want to make this call wearing a hospital gown. He needed to assuage any concern about his own health and safety as quickly as possible. Denzel and Maalyck were out there and in trouble, and they needed to be the priority.

He sat at the table. Denzel's laptop was there, and Kotler didn't have the password.

As if anticipating his need, Nesahor placed Kotler's laptop on the table's surface and moved Denzel's out of the way. Kotler nodded, thanking him, and opened the video call app.

It rang only once before Liz Ludlum answered.

"Dan?" She looked confused, and then relieved. "You're alive!"

"Mostly," Kotler replied, trying to smile. It was good to see her. He had a rush of feelings, somewhat mixed, but they all led him back to the right place. He hadn't realized how much he'd wanted to see her face.

He'd think about that later.

"Roland is in trouble. He and Dr. Maalyck have been abducted by Medo Sarraf, the head of security here."

"Sarraf?" Ludlum said, frowning. "Are you ... are you sure?"

Kotler nodded and told her the whole story. "I couldn't do anything to help them, Liz. I wanted to. I just ..."

"It's ok," she said, her tone soothing and consolatory. "You survived, Dan. That's what you had to do, in the moment. And we have a lead on where they've taken them." She looked up from the camera.

"A lead?" Kotler asked, confused.

There was a sound from offscreen, the camera moved slightly, and in a moment Agent Danielle Brown was leaning in beside Liz. "Dr. Kotler, it's good to see you're alive and ... well, mostly well."

"Agent Brown," Kotler nodded.

"We have a trace on Dr. Maalyck's satellite phone. It was planted in the bag he used to deliver the bronze sword. We're seeing them in the local area, but they seem to be heading back your way."

"Our way?" Nesahor said. His tone was worried.

Kotler thought for a moment. "The chamber of Credne," he said.

"Come again?" Brown asked.

"They're coming here because they need access to that chamber, to open the door to the Otherworld."

Brown and Ludlum exchanged glances. "Dr. Kotler," Brown said, "maybe you need to get a little more rest. You're ..."

"I'm fine," Kotler said. "There are a lot of threads here. But the Ra'id, Medo Sarraf—he and Ammon are both members of a cult. The Alihat Iadida. They're coming here because they have the sword. They're going to use it to try to open Credne's door, in that chamber. The camp is in lockdown, probably under Sarraf's orders."

"You're telling me that an officer in the Egyptian military is behind all this?" Brown asked. He could see the skepticism in her expression.

Kotler shook his head. "I'm telling you he's a member of Alihat Iadida. And he may not be the only one. Whatever this organization is, it's calling the shots here."

"What can we do?" Ludlum asked.

Kotler considered for a moment. "I'm not sure. We need help. Someone we can trust."

"I've made inroads with the State Department," Brown said. "I can request a military contingent. If Sarraf has gone rogue, they'll likely send people to retrieve him."

"Do that," Kotler said. "But Sarraf was heading the military presence in his area. We're a few hours away from the next closest military base. We're going to have to figure a way to keep Sarraf and any of his supporters from doing damage here."

"What do you have in mind?" Brown asked.

Kotler shook his head. "I'm making this up as I go. But I do have one ace up my sleeve."

"What's that?" Ludlum asked.

"The pommel," Kotler replied. "They'll need it if they want to open that door."

Brown huffed. "Let me make sure I have this straight. One of our people handed over one Egyptian artifact to the bad guys, and now you're proposing we give them another one?"

"No," Kotler said. "I'm proposing that I use both artifacts to save the lives of Roland and Martook, as well as everyone here. Because I suspect that Sarraf's men are a lot more loyal to him than to the Egyptian military. And I think the plan all along was to use this camp as a smokescreen. They're going to eliminate everyone when they have what they want."

"What makes you think that?" Brown asked, quietly.

Kotler shook his head. "It's coming to me slowly. But it's that name, *Alihat Iadida*. It means 'New Gods' in Arabic. It's been bugging me since I heard it, and now I know why. This isn't a new cult, just a new name. I originally encountered these people a few years ago, under the name *Diathan Ùra*. Gaelic, for 'New Gods.' Their members were stealing artifacts, mostly for rituals meant to bring them power. They're obsessed with the various pantheons. And they weren't above killing nearly an entire town to further their agenda."

"And you think they'll do the same at that camp?" Brown asked.

"I do," Kotler said. "Unless we stop them."

Brown stared for a moment, then nodded. "Alright. I'll see if we can expedite some help. And you ... you're planning a distraction?"

"Yes," Kotler said. "I'll keep them busy for as long as I can."

"Dan," Ludlum said, and he could see the worry in her expression.

"I'll be fine," he smiled, lying. He wasn't fine now and wasn't sure he'd be any better in a few hours. But he was doing this, and he could see Liz resolve herself to that.

"Take care of yourself, Dr. Kotler," Brown said. "Bring Agent Denzel back to us."

Kotler nodded and closed his laptop, then rose to his feet, a bit unsteady.

Nesahor rushed to help him.

"Do you truly believe Sarraf's men will kill us all?" He asked.

Kotler shook his head. "I'm not sure. But they know he has Agent Denzel. And I don't think it's a coincidence that this place is on lockdown. So we have to assume at least some of Sarraf's men are involved with Alihat Iadida."

"What do we do?" Nesahor asked.

"I need to retrieve that pommel, and then I need to arrange to meet with Sarraf and Ammon when they arrive."

Nesahor nodded and helped Kotler get moving.

CHAPTER TWENTY

Egypt

WHEN THE TRUCK STOPPED AGAIN, Denzel prepared himself for the worst.

After the outcry from their previous stop, they'd been left in the back of the truck for a long while, until finally they heard the driver and passenger doors open and slam, followed by the engine starting. Denzel knew that they'd come here—wherever here was—to retrieve Kotler, and that the likely outcome would have been for all three of them to be shot and left to rot in the mountains somewhere.

But Kotler had escaped. Denzel would recognize a Kotler-fueled cry of rage and frustration anywhere, and he knew in his bones that Kotler had managed to give these men the slip.

So now it was anyone's guess what they intended to do with Denzel and Maalyck. The odds still favored shooting them. But if that was the plan, why not do it here?

Whatever their reasoning, Denzel was grateful to have

more time. He tried to put it to use, to think of some way out of this, but there seemed to be no options.

It was daylight now, and enough light seeped through seams and gaps in the canvas covering the truck to make details visible. Denzel looked to Maalyck and saw that the researcher was drooping. The tourniquet had stopped the bleeding in his leg, but he'd still lost a lot of blood. His pants were soaked in it, as was the shirt tied around his thigh. He would need medical attention soon, or the best-case scenario would be losing the leg.

They were jostled by the road, and Maalyck awoke with a start, wide-eyed and looking frantically around the truck's interior.

"You're ok," Denzel said calmly. "Dr. Maalyck, don't panic. You're ok."

Maalyck looked at him, and after a moment Denzel saw the flicker of recognition.

"Agent Denzel," Maalyck said quietly, as if to himself.

"Yes," Denzel said.

"Where are we going?" Maalyck asked.

Denzel shook his head. "No idea. It's been over an hour, by my estimate."

As if in answer to the question, the truck slowed with the sound of the transmission downshifting. A moment later they stopped, and Denzel could hear voices speaking in Arabic, outside.

"Sarraf's men," Maalyck said. "We are back at the Credne site."

"Back?" Denzel asked, confused. "Why would we ..."

He paused as the realization sunk in.

"Kotler," he said. "Kotler is here."

"How do you know this?" Maalyck asked.

"Because we're both alive," Denzel said. "They're planning

to use us as leverage. They're improvising. Sarraf's men must have alerted him that Kotler was here."

"But why would they need leverage against Dr. Kotler?" Maalyck asked, confused.

Denzel shook his head. "I don't know. There's a lot here that isn't adding up yet."

The truck lurched forward again, and a moment later it stopped, and they heard the doors open once again. Men were talking, and Denzel heard Sarraf's voice giving orders.

The back door of the truck opened, and Denzel and Maalyck blinked into the light of the morning sun.

One of Sarraf's men climbed inside the truck and removed the chains from Denzel and Maalyck, leaving the cuffs in place. He pushed them ahead of him. They were allowed to climb down to the ground, Sarraf's men training rifles on the two of them.

Sarraf and Ammon walked away, leaving Denzel and Maalyck standing at the rear of the truck, under guard.

It was then that Denzel remembered the damned phone.

He had hidden it in his pocket, thinking that Sarraf and Ammon might open the back of the truck at any minute. But as they'd sat there, and Maalyck and his injuries had become the focus of Denzel's attention, as had the knowledge that Kotler had escaped. Denzel had waited for the worst, and the phone had slipped his mind.

A mistake that might cost their lives.

No time to berate himself over that now. He had to assess their situation, start looking for ways out of this. The phone was still in his pocket. If he got the opportunity again, he'd use it.

Denzel looked around the site. He'd seen this area when he'd spoken with Sarraf about Kotler's abduction. Tents served as barracks for the men, and a small trailer sat at one end of the camp, used as an office for Sarraf. Denzel had been in that trailer earlier, meeting with Sarraf to give him details about Kotler's abduction. There were resources in there that Denzel could use, but it was doubtful he'd ever get an opportunity to reach them.

Beyond the trailer was a chain link fence that surrounded the site. Past this, Denzel could see the gates that barred entry to one of the chambers, higher in the mountain. There were more gates like these on half a dozen paths leading into these hills. Normally, they were bustling with activity, with researchers coming and going. At the moment, they were deserted.

Denzel looked toward the research site, in the other direction. Sarraf's men were moving in armed patrols around the perimeter of the camp. Denzel couldn't see the entire perimeter, but he knew what he was looking at.

This place had gone from a research site to a prison.

Or a killing field.

Denzel realized that Sarraf's improvisation was a sign. Grabbing Denzel hadn't been part of a plan, he had just reacted. The fact that he'd taken matters into his own hands, personally taking Denzel under the pretense of arrest, hinted at the man's desperation.

Desperate men, in positions of power, did not like witnesses.

Sarraf was running an end game, from his point of view, and he was willing to make sacrifices. Denzel knew, as sure as if he'd been told, that Sarraf was planning to raze this camp and leave no survivors, once he got what he was after.

Sarraf and Ammon finally returned, and along with two armed guards they escorted Denzel and Maalyck through a gate and up a stone path. After a while, they stopped at one of the gates leading up into the mountain. To Denzel's surprise, two people were waiting for them.

"Dr. Kotler," Sarraf said. He turned to face the other man. "Dr. Nesahor," he said.

Kotler looked a little shaky, but he stepped forward and faced Sarraf. "Ra'id," he said, diplomatically. Denzel could tell, though, that Kotler had his game face on. He looked terrible, but he was acting on a plan.

"How did you escape the cave?" Ammon asked.

"Not now, Ammon," Sarraf said. The man never took his eyes from Kotler's face.

Denzel couldn't quite read people as well as Kotler could, but he knew a power play when he saw one. Sarraf didn't like anyone having an upper hand on him, especially in his own camp. Kotler's escape had upset their plans and their timetable, and it had likely exposed Sarraf and his men. Kotler would surely have made contact with someone outside of the camp. Word would be out. Things were not going well for the Ra'id.

"Tell me why I should not kill you," Sarraf said.

Kotler shook his head. "You're not going to kill me," he said. "I'm the only way that either of you gets what you want. If the Alihat Iadida want to get through Credne's door, you need me to do it."

Ammon stepped forward. He had the bronze sword in his hand, holding it as if he was ready to thrust it into the heart of his enemy.

"We do not need you to open Credne's door," Ammon said, his jaw tight. He raised the sword. "We have the true blade. The key."

Kotler smiled. "I'm afraid you're working with incomplete information," he said. "There's more to unlocking that door than the sword. Even with the real thing, you'll never get in."

Ammon tensed, and Sarraf put a hand on his shoulder. He

turned to Kotler. "What will it take, for you to show us how to open the door?"

Kotler was watching the man's face. "Let them go," he said, nodding to Denzel and Maalyck. "Let everyone go. Clear the camp, and I will show you exactly how to get in."

Sarraf was watching Kotler's face. He nodded and turned to Ammon. He reached for the sword, which Ammon handed over, a baffled expression on his face.

Sarraf held up the sword, inspecting it. He raised it, looking at it in the morning light. He glanced back to Kotler, and then suddenly turned and thrust the blade forward.

"No!" Kotler shouted.

Denzel stood, frozen, looking at the wild insanity in Sarraf's eyes.

He looked down to the blade.

Dr. Maalyck was hunched, his eyes wide, his hands raised to clasp the blade that penetrated his midsection. He looked up to Kotler, then slowly tilted, falling to the ground. Blood was already pooling around him, soaking into the soil.

Kotler tried to rush forward, but one of Sarraf's men slammed him with the butt of his rifle, then aimed his weapon at Kotler's head.

Kotler stumbled, and with Nesahor's help, he managed to stand again. He looked at Maalyck, who lay curled and bleeding on the ground.

Sarraf raised the blade again, this time bringing the point of it to Denzel's throat.

Denzel glared at him.

"Please," Kotler said. "I'll open the door. Just ... please ..."

Sarraf turned and faced Kotler, smiling. He handed the sword back to Ammon who immediately began cleaning the blade with his own shirt, almost frantic in his motions. "You might have damaged it!" he shouted.

"It was made for blood," Sarraf said. "Now, Dr. Kotler, if you will?" He motioned to the gate, beyond which was the path leading to the chamber where Credne's door awaited.

Kotler led the way, and Denzel was shoved along behind him.

CHAPTER TWENTY-ONE

KOTLER STRUGGLED UP THE PATH, his legs still a little rubbery after the previous night's ordeal. His entire body ached, but he was starting to loosen up. Adrenaline was fueling him now.

Martook, he grieved. He didn't dare look back down. Sarraf and his men were driving them forward, and any hesitation was met with brutal assault.

Ammon had stepped in beside Kotler and chatted inanely as they made their way up the stone path.

"This find is really quite remarkable," he said, almost as if he were merely conversing with a colleague, rather than a prisoner. "The Alihat Iadida consider this to be a prime site, in the study of the gods. The door to the Otherworld! Quite exciting."

Kotler said nothing but concentrated on putting one foot in front of the other. He also made a concerted effort not to fling himself at Ammon and dash the man's head against the rocks. It might have been worth it, to take a bullet from Sarraf's men, just to see Ammon bleeding and dying on the ground the way Maalyck was down below. But in that event, Denzel and all the people in the research camp were bound to die as well. Kotler kept moving.

The trek up the mountainside took longer than Kotler would have liked, but by the time they reached the entrance to the Credne vault he was almost grateful for the exercise, as his body limbered, and his strength returned. While his convalescence in the camp had been brief, he'd gotten plenty of fluids and calories. He'd even managed solid food before Nesahor accompanied him to the gate.

Kotler had tried to talk Nesahor out of going. He'd practically ordered the man to stay behind, using all the authority he could muster as the lead at this site. He explained that this was likely to be a one-way trip. Nesahor would be in danger, perhaps even be killed.

"You say that they plan to kill everyone in this camp," Nesahor replied. "I would prefer to die while doing something, rather than be herded and shot like cattle."

Kotler couldn't fault him for that. Though it did raise certain questions about whether they should inform the rest of the camp of what was happening. Ultimately Kotler had decided that it would cause undue panic and, worse, possibly accelerate Sarraf's timetable. He hated leaving anyone ignorant of what was to come—it gnawed at him. He would want to know. He would want to be able to prepare. But time was as much his enemy as it was theirs.

Kotler consoled himself with the hope that he could figure a way to stop all of this and to save all of them. Somehow.

The entrance to the Credne vault was a ragged gap in the mountainside, widened by the research team to allow for easier passage, but otherwise nearly in the same condition as the day it was found. The vault had once been concealed behind a large stone that had to be rolled away, with considerable effort. After the discovery of the entrance, handrails and even stairs and walkways had been installed, as well as runs of cables for light and power. There was a ventilation system pumping fresh air into the space as needed.

They moved deeper into the mountain, and Kotler was taken for a moment by the presence of light.

Looking up he saw that at irregular intervals there were shafts in the stone—some of which were natural chimneys formed as part of the cave system here, and some were apparently carved by whoever built the vault. Embedded in these shafts were large blocks of polished quartz, most about the size of a fist, but some as large as Kotler's head, or perhaps a bit larger.

Kotler had seen shafts such as these before, twenty years earlier, as he and Martook Maalyck—at that time only a young boy—had explored the brass hall of Credne. The builders of this site had turned practically the entire mountain into a temple of sorts, with a network of chambers, vaults, and halls woven into the stone here and sealed away for millennia. The builders were ingenious and innovative in their designs. It made Kotler wonder at their level of technology.

Boring through the stone of the mountain was no mean feat. Doing so by hand wasn't impossible, but it presented challenges that made it seem improbable. All of it required a level of thought and consideration and planning that was beyond anything modern archaeologists attributed to the cultures of the period.

The mechanisms that protected the brass hall and the Credne door were impressive. They hinted at technical proficiency and advancement on a level much higher than anyone would expect. And they hinted at a culture and civilization that operated at a higher level than anything that the archaeological community thought possible.

Kotler was part of a school of thought, within the archaeological community, that believed there was a culture that came before recorded history. A technologically advanced culture with capabilities that seemed like magic to the generations that followed, and a lost civilization, erased from history, with only scant traces remaining.

The gods, Kotler believed, and the mythologies of the world, all stemmed from this lost civilization. There were too many coincidences, too many commonalities for it to be anything else. Somehow a civilization at least equal to the modern world had come and gone and left barely a trace of itself.

Except, of course, for sites such as this one.

The Credne vault was filled with artifacts and objects that were tantalizing in their implications. Kotler would have enjoyed digging in here, examining everything to see how the pieces fit. He wanted to explore and discover.

It would have to wait. He hoped he would live long enough to get the chance.

"The door is this way," Ammon said, his voice tinged with excitement.

Kotler wanted to strangle him. But he couldn't fault him for his enthusiasm. Despite the circumstances, this really was an incredible thing to consider. They were about to open a door that had remained shut for thousands of years. A door that, by all indications, opened to an entire world of new and ancient things to explore.

The Otherworld.

Kotler wasn't sure what this would turn out to be, or what he expected. But it had the weight of something that might alter the course of history, and despite their circumstances that made him excited.

They came to the door. The face of Credne, his eyes closed,

met them like a guardian looming over the chamber. Kotler was shoved toward it by one of Sarraf's men.

"Open it," Sarraf ordered.

Kotler looked back to see Sarraf and Ammon standing in the foreground, with Nesahor to their side. Beyond them, Denzel stood between the two guards, his hands cuffed in front of him.

This was it. Time to get to work.

Kotler huffed and faced them.

"First," he said, "I'm going to need you to turn off the lights."

CHAPTER TWENTY-TWO

SARRAF STEPPED FORWARD, pressing a gun to Denzel's head, ordering Kotler to open the door right that instant or the agent would die.

Kotler held up his hands, preparing to explain, but was relieved when Ammon intervened. "I have seen this," he said to a wary Sarraf. "There is light, from a shaft above." He gestured to the ceiling.

"It is a trick," Sarraf spat. "A distraction."

In the end, it was Dr. Nesahor whose quiet voice convinced Sarraf. "He is correct," Nesahor said. "We discovered the shaft years ago, though we never ascertained its purpose. It opens when Credne's face is pressed inward."

Sarraf studied Nesahor for a long moment, and to Kotler's surprise he nodded and ordered one of his men to go and shut off the lights. The guard ran out of the chamber to the circuit box just inside the cave entrance.

When the lights snapped off, an eerie silence also fell upon the room. The ventilation fans stopped, the hum of the motors dying as the fan blades spun down. Before the lights were shut off, Sarraf turned on a flashlight, and the wide beam of it provided enough light to allow everyone to see. He was still aiming his weapon at Denzel's head.

Kotler turned, examining the door, the ceiling, the floor. He reached out and pushed the face inward, and there was the sound of stone grinding and moving.

"I need it to be dark," Kotler said over his shoulder.

There was a pause, and he glanced back at Sarraf. The man shook his head at first, then said, "If you try to escape, I will shoot him." He turned to Denzel. "If you move, I will kill you without hesitation."

Denzel nodded, saying nothing.

"This is necessary," Kotler said.

"There is a shaft for light to come into the room," Ammon assured Sarraf, pointing to the high ceiling. "I have seen it."

Sarraf scowled and nodded, then turned off the flashlight.

It took a moment for Kotler's eyes to adjust, but soon the stream of morning sunlight seemed as bright as any flashlight beam. He glanced up at the ceiling. High above them, he surmised, was another polished quartz porthole. It allowed light to enter, and perhaps even magnified that light.

"I need the sword," Kotler said.

Ammon handed it to him without hesitation, and Kotler hefted it.

He could end Ammon right now. He might even be able to reach Sarraf before being gunned down. But Denzel would surely be killed in the scuffle.

Kotler reluctantly let the fantasy pass, and held the sword by the hilt, balancing the flat of the blade against the fingers of his left hand. He held it parallel to the floor, aligned it, and then pressed it into the opening in Credne's mouth.

He pushed, using an even and steady pressure, not forcing it. In return, he felt and heard the ancient mechanism engage, though nothing seemed to happen in the room around them.

Ammon was leaning closer, and Kotler could hear his excited breathing. He resisted the urge to shiver.

There was a pause, and Ammon rose. "It did not work!"

Kotler shook his head. "It worked. It just isn't finished."

"Finished?" Ammon scoffed.

Kotler reached into his pocket and removed the pommel, holding it up for Ammon to see in the light from the shaft.

"What is this?" Ammon asked.

"The piece you were missing," Kotler replied.

He turned to the sword and raised the pommel, aligning it so that he could press it into place and turn it. With a click, it locked onto the hilt of the sword, and Kotler stepped away.

The light from the shaft struck the jewel in the pommel's center and cast a crimson ray to the floor. Kotler and Ammon both bent to inspect it.

"A map?" Ammon asked in awe.

"To the Otherworld," Kotler said, his voice just as quiet.

He knelt and ran his fingers over the texture of the floor.

It was indeed a map, and in combination with the pattern etched into the floor it created a sort of bas relief, almost like a 3D projection.

Kotler recognized it.

"This is a contour map of these mountains," he said quietly. "Here," he said, pointing to a particular spot. "This is where we are. This, here, is the brass hall. And these are the other sites we've discovered. These ... we haven't located these. This map is the key to the entire site." He shook his head. "Incredible."

"But what of the Otherworld?" Ammon asked.

Kotler detected the impatience, the growing frustration.

"Give me a moment," he said.

Sarraf yanked Denzel forward, forcing him to his knees. He

pressed the gun to Denzel's head hard enough that Denzel was forced to tilt away from it. "You have ten minutes, Dr. Kotler. Open the door in that time, or I will shoot Agent Denzel in front of you."

Kotler held up his hands. "I'm doing my best! Please, give me time!"

"Ten minutes!" Sarraf shouted. "Beginning now."

Kotler turned back to the map, studying it, trying to work out the message that the builders had intended.

Why a map?

The door seemed the most obvious means for gaining access to whatever the Otherworld turned out to be. Credne's face acted as a sort of guardian for it. The sword was the key. But the door remained firmly shut, and before them, all they really had was a macabre vision of Credne impaled on the sword. Death, then.

Death.

Kotler looked up to Credne's face. If this was how the god had died, in some unrecorded bit of mythology, then this door really should lead to the Otherworld. If that was the case, however, then why would the builders need the map? What message were they ...

It hit Kotler then, sudden and bright.

A message. A pattern.

He looked again at the map on the floor and ignored the contours, focusing instead on the positioning of the landmarks. He was looking at the patterns.

Ignoring the contours of the landscape, the placement of each of the sites in the region formed an overall pattern that Kotler recognized. Three lines—acute triangles, really—lay in parallel to each other, oriented toward three primary locations.

"Awen," Kotler whispered.

"Awen?" Ammon replied.

Kotler indicated the pattern he was seeing, tracing it with his finger.

"Here, do you see? These sites are all aligned to a pattern. Do you ... I need a piece of paper and a pen, something to draw with."

"Here," Nesahor said, patting his pocket and producing a small notepad and a pencil. He handed this to Kotler, who nodded appreciatively.

Kotler sketched a rough approximation of what he was seeing.

He showed the drawing to Ammon and to Sarraf. "Three rays, you see? They represent three rays of light, or three flames. Those three circles represent three gods—a holy trinity. The two outer rays represent male and female. The center ray represents balance. Sort of a Celtic yin and yang. This symbol is supposed to be Neo-Druidic, traced back to the 9th century. But it may have roots even earlier than that."

"What does it mean?" Ammon asked quietly.

Kotler considered, thinking about the symbol in context. "This map is supposed to lead us to the Otherworld," he said. "It clearly reveals the secret chambers of this site." He looked at it again, holding the paper in the light.

"Look," he said, after a moment.

Ammon leaned in.

"Three deities," Kotler said. "Three was a significant number in Druidic culture. These rays represent the balance of the sexes, but they also represent mind, body, and spirit. Also earth, sea, and sky. But notice, here ..." he pointed to the drawing. "All three rays point to the center deity."

"Is that significant?" Ammon asked.

"I think it's what we're looking for," Kotler replied. "I think this is where we'll find the Otherworld. Not here. Not this door. This," he motioned to the door before them, and to the chamber itself. "This is another decoy. A ... a map room. Here," he said, pointing to the floor. He put his finger on the spot where the middle deity would be, represented by one of the primary sites on the map. "We have to go here."

Sarraf shoved Denzel to the floor and ordered his man to cover him. The other guard had returned now, and Sarraf stepped forward, bending over the map, studying it. "I recognize this," he said. "That area is difficult and treacherous. It has not yet been opened to exploration." He straightened. "If you are lying ..."

"I'm not," Kotler said. "That's the place. If the Alihat Iadida wants to gain access to the Otherworld, it's going to happen there."

Sarraf shook his head. "This will require significant resources," he replied. "It will expose us."

At that moment, Dr. Nesahor stepped forward. Kotler expected to see the guards raise their weapons, or for Sarraf himself to react. But Nesahor was allowed to move freely. "It is a risk we must take," he said to Sarraf.

He looked to Kotler, who still knelt beside the map, confused. Slowly the truth dawned on him.

"For the order," Nesahor said then, and turned to Sarraf. "Make the arrangements."

CHAPTER TWENTY-THREE

FBI Headquarters, Manhattan

Lᴜᴅʟᴜᴍ sᴛᴏᴏᴅ with Agent Brown in what they were calling the war room—a control room allowing remote viewing of the actions happening in Egypt. They were guests of the US Department of State, on a floor of their New York offices. In addition to their FBI credentials, they wore guest badges that gave them access to select areas. Ludlum was fidgeting with this badge, hanging from a lanyard around her neck, watching as a contingent of US operatives worked in conjunction with the Egyptian military, in a raid on the Credne site.

The operatives were moving quietly through the hills, and the scenes on the myriad of screens in the room came from body cam and helmet cam feeds. She could hear radio chatter, some in English but most in Arabic.

Personnel in the room were communicating with the agents in the field, issuing orders and coordinating the operation.

Ludlum watched, nervous and worried.

She leaned over to whisper to Agent Brown. "What should we expect to see?"

"They're moving on the camp soon. We're seeing our guys, but Egyptian operatives are surrounding the site. From what I've heard, Ra'id Sarraf's men have everyone in the camp locked down, basically hostages. So they're having to do this very carefully."

"Any sign of Dan? Or Roland?"

Brown shook her head. "Not yet."

On the main screen, things started moving. Ludlum watched the jostled, shaking image as the operative behind it sprinted down into the valley, sliding at times down gullies in the hillside. He took cover as another man appeared on screen, carrying a rifle and wearing the uniform of the Egyptian military.

"How do they tell them apart?" Ludlum asked. "The bad guys from the good guys?"

"Good guys are wearing insignia on their sleeves," Brown replied.

Onscreen, the Egyptian soldier passed by without noticing the American operative, and within seconds the operative sprang out of hiding and took the man down. There were no shots fired, and not even a peep out of the enemy. He was gagged and trussed up, and then dragged back into the hills.

The view switched to another helmet cam, and a similar attack was in progress.

The plan, as far as Ludlum could determine, was for the Americans to be the initial incursion force, cutting into the enemy like a scalpel so that the Egyptian contingent could come in and clean up with minimal risk to the civilians. The action they'd just witnessed was just one of dozens along the perimeter. The operation was well under way.

Reports were coming from all directions, as far as Ludlum

could determine, and she was impressed that anyone could follow and coordinate it all. It seemed to her to be chaos. Her training, her temperament, made her want to straighten out all of the lines and narrow things down, to find a single cause at the root of everything. This was a different way of thinking, like solving puzzles in parallel. It was exciting but exhausting to her.

"Agent Brown, Dr. Ludlum." Assistant Secretary Dale Craft approached from the floor. He was coordinating the cooperative operation, on behalf of the State Department, and had arranged for the two of them to be here. "We have some news. The raid has been successful in removing the rogue element. The camp has been reclaimed."

"Any casualties?" Brown asked. "Any sign of our people?"

Craft shook his head. "There are some injuries, but we're still getting the reports. No sign of Agent Denzel or Dr. Kotler. However, we've gotten word that Ra'id Sarraf and some of his men left the site in a military transport about an hour ago, before our team arrived."

"Left?" Ludlum asked. "Where did they go?"

Craft shook his head. "No idea yet. We're checking satellite footage now. Shouldn't be long. The Egyptian government is being very cooperative. They're not happy about one of their own being behind this. They've allowed us to bypass a lot of the red tape."

He left, and Ludlum turned her attention back to activity onscreen. She had secretly held on to the hope that she would see Kotler's face appear there, as he was rescued. Now she wasn't sure if she'd ever see him again.

"Come on," Brown said, tugging at her arm.

"Where are we going?" Ludlum replied, following reluctantly.

"Commissary," Brown said, holding up the visitor's badge. "It's one of the places we have access to. And it has donuts."

They took an elevator to the ground floor, and into a corridor ending at a set of glass doors that opened into the commissary. The space overlooked a courtyard of lush, green plants. The commissary encircled the courtyard with seating and a serving area. Brown went straight for a cart of donuts, followed by the coffee station.

Ludlum usually avoided donuts, but this was a special case. She chose something with nuts on it, in an attempt to at least pretend she was eating something healthy.

They sat at one of the tables overlooking the courtyard, coffee and donuts before them. Ludlum picked at hers, eating small pinches at a time.

"Call me Dani," Brown said to her as she dunked a chunk of donut in her coffee.

"I'm ... what?" Ludlum replied.

"Dani," Brown said. "Short for Danielle."

"I know, I just ... why are you telling me to call you Dani?"

Brown shrugged and popped the coffee-soaked bit of donut into her mouth. She swallowed and smiled. "It just seems like you need a friend more than an FBI agent. So ..." she patted her chest. "Dani."

Ludlum blinked, and smiled, then mimicked the gesture. "Liz," she said.

Brown nodded. "They're going to find him, you know."

Ludlum nodded. "I know. I'm just prepared for finding in him in bad condition."

Brown sipped her coffee, blowing on it to cool it a bit. "Good. Because honestly, that's a likely outcome. It's hard to hear, I know. But we may not be able to save them."

"I know," Ludlum said.

"But we stopped the bad guys," Brown said.

Ludlum thought about this. The truth was, they hadn't entirely stopped the bad guys. Not yet. Sarraf was still out there, with a contingent of armed men and an agenda they could only guess at. No one knew for sure what he was really after, or how far he would take things. He may already have gotten what he wanted and escaped, for all they knew.

"It's out of our hands for now," Ludlum said, sipping her own coffee. She hesitated then, and said, "Can I change the subject? I mean, it's sort of related."

"Shoot," Brown replied.

Ludlum nodded. "Ok, I've been thinking about the question you raised. About Historic Crimes. About Dan. You were wondering about the department."

Brown was watching her and didn't speak, but nodded.

"I'm wondering, too," Ludlum said, her voice involuntarily going quieter. "I'm wondering who approved all of it. Who is behind it? So ... I started looking." She glanced away as she said this, looking to the green of the courtyard.

Brown was dunking another bit of donut into her coffee. "And ... did you find anything?"

Ludlum shook her head. "Not yet. This took precedence," she waved a hand, encompassing the State Department building. "I was looking over our charter, trying to find who wrote it and who commissioned everything. But so far, nothing."

"I'm not surprised," Brown said. "These things usually go through so many channels, there's no way to know who came up with the initial idea. For all we know this was sitting there waiting to be approved when Denzel and Kotler came along. Right place, right time."

Ludlum nodded. "I can see how that might be it. And maybe it is. But I can't get it out of my head. Something about all of this isn't quite right. I had always thought of Historic Crimes as a sort of task force. But a task force has a specific objective and a timeline. Historic Crimes ... it's a whole new division of the FBI. The charter is broad. The conditions a case has to meet to be considered under our purview ... well, they're pretty wide open."

"So what do you think that means?" Brown asked.

Ludlum shook her head. "I'm not sure. Not yet. But ... I was hoping maybe you could help me find out."

"Me?" Brown asked. "Why me?"

"It was your question, originally. You found all of this suspicious. You had the gut instinct. And, well, you have more reach than I do, when it comes to accessing records we'll need."

"So you want me to help you get into FBI files, above your clearance."

Ludlum sighed and leaned back. "No, I guess not. You're right, that's probably a bad idea."

"I didn't say that," Brown replied. "I'm just making sure I'm defining the roles properly." She leaned forward, her voice just above a whisper. "I can't investigate this myself," she said. "Not the way I need to. But I've wanted to dig into this. I don't think Denzel or Kotler are into anything here, but my gut tells me that someone out there is playing a game. The boys aren't seeing it. Maybe they don't want to see it. So it's up to us."

Ludlum listened and watched. "And what about you?"

"What about me?" Brown replied.

"I want to uncover this, whatever it is, because I care about Dan, and about Agent Denzel," Ludlum said. "What's driving you?"

Brown shook her head. "I care about them, too. But you're right. I have my own reasons. I want to know who pays my check, and who calls the shots I take. I want to know that I'm working for the good guys, and that I'm not part of something ... I dunno ... dark? Sinister?"

"The good guys," Ludlum said, thinking. She sipped her

coffee again and nodded. "Ok. So we're going to assume that we're on that side. And that Roland and Dan are, too."

"Maybe," Brown said. "We can't just make assumptions. We should vet them. Clear them. Then keep digging."

Ludlum considered this, then nodded. "You're right. If I were investigating this as a forensics case, that's exactly what I'd have to do. Ok, we'll start there."

"And I'll get you any information you need. As much as I can," Brown said. "I'll do some digging on my own, but I'll have to be a bit more careful. I think you can make more progress on this than I can. No one will be watching you, if you limit how you dig. Plus you have contacts outside of the FBI, from your NYPD days. You're perfect for this."

That made Ludlum pause. She put the coffee cup on the table and pressed the palms of her hands against the flat surface, leaning forward. "Dani," she said, "was this your plan all along? Get me intrigued? Get me working on this?"

Brown leaned back and brought her coffee to her lips. She popped the last of her donut into her mouth and washed it down. She nodded to Ludlum's partially eaten donut.

"You going to finish that?" she asked.

Ludlum shook her head. Brown picked up the donut and started breaking it into chunks, and Ludlum thought that maybe she had her answer.

CHAPTER TWENTY-FOUR

Egypt

KOTLER AND DENZEL were both cuffed and secured in the back of a military transport—one of two vehicles on their way to the Otherworld site. Their truck was filled with armed men, presumably Sarraf's most trusted soldiers. There was no chance to speak, much less make an escape, and so the two of them rode in silence.

The second truck had fewer personnel. It was loaded with the equipment they might need, once they got to the site. The location was remote, and the terrain was rough. There was some indication, from the rough map they had, that they might have to do some climbing and excavation.

Ammon and Nesahor were in the second truck. Sarraf was in the cab of the one Kotler and Denzel were in. They were all on their way to a spot that would be the perfect location to dump the bodies of two Americans.

The ride was rough, and they were jostled quite a bit as the truck drove over terrain that would cripple most vehicles. They were rising higher into the mountains here, and there were no roads.

Even if he and Denzel managed to escape, Kotler thought, they might never make it back to civilization.

They'd been traveling for a couple of hours, by Kotler's estimate, when finally the truck slowed and stopped, maneuvering into position through a series of turns and reverses. When the engine stopped, the soldiers filed out, closing the door behind them.

Kotler and Denzel were left chained to their seats as Sarraf's men exited the truck. The soldiers would do the work of setting up equipment and preparing the site. Kotler could hear Sarraf shouting orders in Arabic.

"Any ideas about how we get out of this?" Denzel asked.

Kotler shook his head. "Not a one. I was counting on us opening the Credne door, back at the camp. I was hoping to buy us time."

"Time for what?" Denzel asked.

"For rescue," Kotler replied. "I've been in contact with Liz and Agent Brown. They were arranging for the Egyptian authorities to send help. But I didn't count on us moving from the site."

"Any idea what their ETA was?" Denzel asked.

Kotler shook his head. "They were just making the arrangements when Sarraf and Ammon arrived back at camp." Kotler thought about Maalyck, laying on the ground in a pool of blood. Kotler's heart ached for his friend, but at the moment he had troubles enough of his own.

He looked up to see Denzel staring at the floor.

"What about you?" Kotler asked.

Denzel shook his head. "No ideas about escape, but I'm

thinking your plan to stall and buy time might still be a good one."

"How so?"

"If Brown managed to get the Egyptian authorities moving, it means she went to the State Department. They'll likely use satellites to track us from the Credne site to here. And ..." he tapped one of the pockets of his pants. "I still have the satellite phone. So ..."

"So if we can keep progress to a minimum, they may still get here in time," Kotler said.

"Think you can make it look like you're working on this and stall at the same time?" Denzel asked.

Kotler considered. "With Ammon and Nesahor here, it's going to be tricky. They're both archaeologists. They'll be able to tell if I'm blowing smoke. I think I may have more insight into Druidic customs, which may help. But it's dicey."

"Do whatever you can," Denzel said. "I'll see if I can help drag us along."

"Be careful," Kotler warned. "Sarraf is pretty intent on using you as leverage against me."

Denzel locked eyes with him. "It may come down to letting him do what he's going to do."

Kotler shook his head and was about to say something when the door to the truck swung open. He and Denzel turned to see two of Sarraf's men climb inside. They unlocked the chains and shoved Kotler and Denzel out of the truck.

They managed to get safely to the rocky terrain outside without falling face-first from the truck, and Kotler looked around to get an idea of the place. They were high in the mountains, on a flat ridge that overlooked a sheer drop into a crag below. He pictured the map from the Credne vault. This place was several miles east of the main camp, and the mountains became more predominant here. There were no signs of paths or other means of egress. They would have to rappel from here.

"We have located the most likely entrance," Ammon said. He was holding a map, folded to display their current location and marked with grease pencil. "Here," Ammon said, pointing with one finger. He looked to Kotler. "There is a large stone there, on a ridge. It appears similar to the entrance to the Credne vault." He said this last with a grin, and his demeanor was that of a colleague, rather than a captor. Kotler despised the man, but for the moment he would have to play into his delusions.

"Remarkable," Kotler said, filling his voice with awe.

He turned to Dr. Nesahor. "When the vault was discovered, what methods were used to open it?"

Nesahor was quiet, watching Kotler, and for a moment Kotler wondered if the man recognized that this was all a distraction. Could he read through Kotler's ruse?

Nesahor shook his head. "It required a crane and several workers. The entry was then widened by hand, to allow for equipment to be brought in."

Kotler considered this and shook his head. "I don't think we could get a crane down there, though we might be able to reach it from up top, lift the stone out of the way."

"We do not have a crane," Ammon said, then smiled. "But we do have another way."

"What's that?" Kotler asked.

Ammon nodded to the transport. "There is a winch on the front of this truck. We will attach it to the stone and pull it free."

Kotler's eyes widened. "That stone has to weigh at least a thousand pounds! Can the winch handle that?"

"It will handle it," Sarraf said, stepping forward. "We need only move it a few inches, and then allow it to fall."

Kotler wanted to object, to suggest some other plan, but he couldn't think of a way to justify it. He worried that it would become apparent he was stalling. Instead, he nodded, and Sarraf turned and ordered his men to get to work.

Kotler was kept away from Denzel during this time. His cuffs were removed, but Denzel's remained, and he was held under close guard.

Kotler was working an angle that had its drawbacks but might give him more opportunities. He was annoyed by Ammon and despised both him and Nesahor, but he kept his feelings in check. Kotler talked to them as colleagues, discussing potential risks to both the workers and the site, offering suggestions for how to proceed, once the stone was removed. He even engaged in animated discussions with Ammon about what it meant, that the Druids had such a strong presence in this region. How had their culture influenced the locals? Had they even made contact? There were mysteries and questions here that Kotler had a legitimate interest in uncovering, and so it made it that much easier to continue the ruse.

In effect, Kotler was ingratiating himself to them, to get them thinking of him as an ally, and to lower their guard.

It seemed to work with the two archaeologists, but Sarraf was a tougher sell. He was naturally suspicious, and never let Kotler forget that he was their prisoner. He was belligerent at times and quick to fall back on menace as his tool of influence. The threat to Denzel's life loomed over everything.

Even Sarraf started coming around, however. In small doses, at least. Kotler found that as he pushed the limits of his latitude at this site, he had fewer and fewer restrictions. He was able to move freely, and he had access to tools and resources that would have been forbidden to him earlier. The strategy was working.

It wasn't much, but it was more than he'd had just a couple

of hours earlier. He wasn't sure if there was anything within his grasp that might aid in their escape, however.

They drove the transport to the edge of the ravine, and one of Sarraf's men rappelled down to the stone. The winch was activated, and the cable was fed to the man below. Kotler stood next to the edge and watched as the man drove pitons into the boulder, snaking the feed line through the hooks and securing it to itself before ascending back to the plateau.

"Are we ready?" Ammon asked, his voice filled with barely contained anticipation.

"We will use the winch to lift the stone," Sarraf said. "We will then sever the line and allow the stone to fall. Prepare to rappel to the rock shelf."

Ammon nodded and motioned for Kotler to follow him. They stepped up to the back of the equipment truck, where several harnesses had been laid out. Kotler had done his share of rock climbing in the past and quickly pulled on his harness, securing the buckles and checking the straps and carabiners. Everything checked.

Ammon seemed to have trouble, and Kotler assisted, ignoring the man's nodding and thank-yous and focusing on the task. He toyed with the idea of sabotaging Ammon's harness somehow, but it would look immediately suspicious. Denzel would pay for a trick like that, and Kotler let it pass.

Nesahor joined them. "I will remain here. But you'll wear this helmet camera." He handed Kotler a helmet with a small camera mounted to the top.

Kotler strapped it on, and Nesahor lifted a small portable display, showing Kotler the image. Anywhere Kotler's head turned, the screen reflected what he saw.

"Two of Sarraf's men will accompany you," Nesahor said.

Kotler nodded. "I'd like Agent Denzel to be there as well," he said.

It was a gamble. A play. But as Kotler suspected, it didn't pay off.

"Dr. Kotler, please," Nesahor smiled. "Do not insult me. Agent Denzel will remain here, as insurance that you do not betray us."

Kotler smiled, though it was a bit forced. "I had to try."

"If you deem that you must try anything else," Nesahor replied, "I will have Sarraf kill your friend and send his body down to you."

Kotler studied Nesahor. The man meant it, and for the first time, Kotler realized that Nesahor may have been playing a similar strategy, lulling Kotler into complacency through professional camaraderie. His body language told Kotler that the man wouldn't hesitate to kill him, however. The threat was clear.

Kotler nodded and followed Sarraf's men who guided him to the cliff's edge.

"Down we go!" Ammon said.

Kotler found himself hoping that Ammon's line would snap. But there was little hope in that. Kotler would have to continue to play along until an opportunity presented itself.

He did have some resources, though.

In among the items he'd gained access to, there had been a multi-tool. It was effectively a pair of pliers that could fold open to reveal a set of other small tools, including a knife blade. The whole thing folded neatly into something resembling a pocket knife, and Kotler had been able to palm this and slip it into a pocket. Now, as he was led to the cliff's edge, he patted himself as if verifying that his harness as secure, and he felt the lump of the multi-tool in his pocket. He could reach in and grab it at any time.

He wasn't sure how this would help him, but he at least felt better knowing it was there.

"Down we go," Kotler repeated, blowing out a breath and steadying his nerves. Moments later he was rappelling down, his feet bounding from the cliff face, toward the gateway to the Otherworld.

CHAPTER TWENTY-FIVE

THE SOLDIERS SHOVED Denzel ahead of them until they reached the transport. He could see the winch line extending over the edge of the rock, pulled taut and ready to lift the stone from its place. Down below, Kotler and the others would land on the shelf of rock where the stone rested. The plan was to winch the rock upward, and then one of the men below would sever the line and let the stone fall away.

There was little wiggle room in that plan that Denzel felt either he or Kotler could exploit. Which meant he'd have to keep watching, keep listening, keep hoping that something opened up.

The soldiers shoved him into the side of the transport's driver-side door, and one of them held a weapon on Denzel while the other removed one of Denzel's cuffs and clipped it to the support of the truck's mirror. They left him then, joining the rest of their squad.

Sarraf approached, a smirk on his face. "When Dr. Kotler has delivered what we need, I will enjoy killing the both of you.

Denzel nodded. "So there never was any chance we were making it out of this alive," he said.

Sarraf laughed. "Of course not."

"What if you end up needing Kotler again?" Denzel asked. "He's pretty good at figuring things like this out. He could be useful somewhere else."

Sarraf studied him, then shook his head. "There are other archaeologists. Kotler was a convenience, not a necessity. And now he has become a liability."

He stepped past Denzel and opened the truck's door, forcing Denzel to step forward. It was a show of his disdain for Denzel, and his confidence that the agent had no chance of escape, even if he could take down Sarraf in this moment.

Sarraf fished around inside the truck and then straightened, holding up a small device. A remote, Denzel realized, to operate the truck's winch. "Soon," Sarraf smiled, closing the driver's door before moving away to join his men.

The timetable was accelerating. Denzel and Kotler couldn't afford to wait for rescue. Denzel started looking around, trying to decide what options he had, even if they were terrible.

The mirror for the transport was attached to a bent and shaped length of flattened steel, secured to the door by two bolts. Though the transport was armored, it was skinned in aluminum, with the plating on the inside. It was possible that the mirror was bolted to the skin of the vehicle, rather than the steel armor beneath. So it might be possible to yank one of those bolts free, to create a gap that he could slip the cuffs out of.

Which was all well and good, but there was zero chance he could do it without making a lot of noise, including the sound of the gun that would put a bullet in his skull.

The door was unlocked, but Denzel was cuffed at an angle that made it impossible to get inside. And even if he could get inside ... then what? There were no weapons, that he could determine, and no keys. It was pretty bare bones—steering wheel, manual stick shift, brake and accelerator pedals, parking brake. Denzel noted with some alarm that the parking brake wasn't engaged, which meant that the only thing keeping the truck from rolling was the fact that it was in gear. He wasn't too keen on being dragged down into the ravine below by several tons of military transport. He might attempt to get inside just to pull that brake.

So much for the truck.

At his feet, some of the stones might be useful, particularly for smashing the truck's window. But as weapons, he'd have to be close up and have the element of surprise, not to mention two free hands, to really do any good.

What he needed was a distraction. And he wasn't likely to get it.

Except ...

He realized he'd been hearing the buzz for a moment now. A sound, ranging through the mountains, distant but getting closer. He looked toward the west and saw four small objects in the sky. Birds, but not the feathered kind.

He smiled.

Someone among Sarraf's men noticed the approaching helicopters as well and shouted an alert. The men scrambled, taking cover and raising weapons.

In moments, all were engaged in a heavy firefight.

Denzel ducked, though there was nowhere for him to go. Cuffed where he was, he was out in the open and in the hot zone. If he couldn't get free, he might take friendly fire.

The helicopters were banking and making passes, door gunners laying suppression fire and dropping smoke. The whole scene brought back memories for Denzel, combat in the desert. It adrenalized him, and his training came screaming back to the foreground of his brain. His first order of business had to be freeing himself. His options opened up from there.

He stooped and picked up one of the heavy stones at his feet and raised this high over his head. He brought it down hard, again and again, on the seam between the steel support of the mirror and the metal of the door.

At the same time, he gripped the frame with his cuffed hand, and put his weight into it, practically hanging from it until finally, he saw the skin of the door pucker and tear, the bolt pulling free.

He dropped the stone then and yanked downward on the support with both hands, putting all of his weight into it. The gap opened, and he was able to slip the cuff free.

Bullets rained onto the site from above, plowing the stone and soil of the plateau, adding dust and debris to the suppressive smoke being launched from the choppers. Sarraf's men took cover and returned fire. Denzel, having nowhere else to hide, flung the truck door open and dove inside. He slammed the door closed behind him and got down into the floorboard, praying that there was enough steel surrounding him to provide protection. He heard several rounds thunk into the side of the truck, like large hail on a tin roof.

In a lull in the battle he looked up, peering out of the driver's window. The scene was carnage. Several of Sarraf's men were down, bleeding and dying on the rock. More were still hunkered behind the second transport, or behind equipment, firing back at the helicopters. Smoke swirled around the whole scene, making it difficult to see everything, but it was clear that Sarraf's soldiers were losing this fight. It was only a matter of time before ground support came in to clean up this mess.

Denzel wondered about Kotler and the others below. They would be waiting for the stone to be lifted but would surely hear and see evidence of the attack happening above. Would Sarraf's men kill Kotler? If they'd had that as a general order, once Kotler's usefulness came to an end, they might decide to cut their losses and take him out. Or Ammon, in a fit of zeal, might do it for them.

Denzel couldn't think about that now. As he peered through the smoke, he saw a figure approaching, walking for all the world as if nothing were happening around him. Trails of bullets rose in plumes to either side of him, dust and debris arcing behind his back, like the wings of a fallen archangel. The angel of death.

Sarraf.

He raised a pistol and fired as he walked. Denzel ducked back into the floor of the transport as bullets pinged from armor plating and pierced the glass of the door, eventually sending shards of it raining down on him. He covered his head and face with his hands.

He prepared for the inevitable, shifting his position, laying with his legs scrunched against the door.

The door of the transport was yanked open, and Sarraf stood over him, aiming his weapon.

Denzel kicked upward just as Sarraf fired, and the bullet ricocheted within the truck's interior until embedding in the passenger seat. Denzel used Sarraf's surprise, rolling forward to grab the man's arm and slam it against the door frame.

Sarraf fought back, landing several well-placed punches. Denzel was dazed but held on.

He doubled his effort and yanked Sarraf forward into the cab of the truck. Denzel clutched the loose handcuff in his right fist, and used it as a set of brass knuckles, punching Sarraf in the temple, the jaw, the neck.

It was having an impact. Sarraf wobbled a bit, blood trickling down the side of his face from deep lacerations. But he quickly regained his wits. He struggled now to tilt the barrel of his weapon, to aim for Denzel's torso. One shot would be all it would take.

Rather than fight, Denzel used Sarraf's own strength against him, pulling Sarraf forward and throwing the man off balance. Denzel twisted, pressing Sarraf into the gap between the seat and door frame.

Another punch using the cuffs, and Denzel was now on top of the man. Sarraf had dropped the gun in the struggle but was scrambling for it now, pushing against Denzel's chin, and kicking wildly.

His head struck the gear shift, and Denzel felt a sick stab in his gut as he realized that they were moving.

He looked up, out of the open driver's side door, and saw the edge of the cliff moving toward the rear of the truck, and then the horizon tilted.

Sarraf managed to get his hand on the pistol then and turned it on Denzel just as the front end of the transport dipped, and they went with it over the edge, falling toward the ravine below.

CHAPTER TWENTY-SIX

KOTLER, Ammon, and the two soldiers hugged the cliff face as Armageddon landed on the men above.

The sound of helicopters banking and diving, laying fire on the plateau, echoed into the ravine, amplified by the stone and nearly deafening them.

For a long moment, everyone on the rock shelf forgot they were enemies and busied themselves with taking cover. After a while, however, it became clear that they were in no danger here. Not from gunfire. Not from above.

The soldiers drew their weapons and ordered Kotler to kneel.

Ammon stepped away from Kotler then, standing behind the soldiers, watching.

So much for camaraderie, Kotler mused.

And then he laughed. Loud, but not manic. The tension of all of this, the worry that they might kill Denzel and then kill him, it all fell away. Right now, Kotler was fully aware that he was about to die, and it didn't bother him.

He knelt. He tilted his head downward. He laughed.

The soldiers stepped forward, apparently deciding they should shoot him at close range, to be sure to end him quickly. They would dump him over the edge, where he'd become a part of the landscape here.

Fitting, in its way, Kotler thought. More bones in proximity to an archaeological site of profound importance. Kotler couldn't for the life of him think of a better way to go, and suddenly he wanted it. If he had to die, at least he'd die knowing that he'd helped Alihat Iadida—the *New Gods*—in this particular raid on history. And he'd become a part of the story of this place. It was a fitting and honorable end.

"Look out!" Ammon shouted, and Kotler realized he'd said it in Arabic, out of panic.

Kotler glanced up, along with the soldiers, and couldn't quite make sense of what he was seeing.

There was a truck driving toward them.

Not driving, he suddenly realized. *Falling!*

Despite his earlier acceptance of the inevitable, Kotler suddenly felt the driving need to *live*. He rolled back onto his heels and sprang to his feet. He then leapt out from the shelf, into the void of the ravine.

The rope was still attached to his harness. He'd been in the process of untethering himself, after assisting Ammon and one of the soldiers in the descent, and he clutched at the line now, swinging from it in an arc that carried him away from the cliff face.

He looked back just as the truck smashed headfirst into the stone that blocked the Otherworld entrance, in an orgy of mangled metal and fractured rock, accompanied by a cacophony of noise that momentarily blotted out the sounds of combat from above. For a moment, as Kotler swung out to his apex and the motion of the truck ceased abruptly, there was the sense of time stopping, and the moment stretching. As Kotler's momentum resumed, however, so did that of the truck. It slowly tilted, like a felled red oak, falling to the side, directly on top of Ammon and the two soldiers.

The men screamed and tried to scramble and escape. One of the soldiers teetered on the edge of the shelf before losing his balance and falling into the gap below. He too was still attached to the rope, but apparently hadn't had the wits to take hold of it. Kotler lost sight of him.

The other soldier and Ammon disappeared under the heap of smoldering rubble from the truck.

Kotler's arc finally brought him back to the cliff face, and he absorbed the impact with his legs, stopping himself and dangling with his feet planted on the rock, his gloved hands gripping the rope. He watched as the truck's momentum caused it to roll, carrying it slowly over the edge, leaving behind only bits of rubble, smashed auto parts and chips of stone mingled with blood and gore.

Ammon and the other soldier were nothing but smears on the shelf now. Kotler couldn't say he would miss them.

From above, Kotler heard more sounds of combat, though the pace of it seemed far less frenetic. It was the sound of a battle being won.

He glanced up to see what he could make out, and what mess he'd be climbing into.

He spotted a someone dangling above him a few feet below the ridgeline, and recognized the animated, cursing figure immediately.

"Roland?" Kotler called.

Denzel was clutching one of the ropes, possibly Ammon's, and hugging the cliff face, struggling for a foothold. "Kotler," he shouted down, and even at this distance, Kotler could see his partner's relief. "Fancy meeting you here."

CHAPTER TWENTY-SEVEN

Up top, the smoke was clearing, and Sarraf's men were being taken into custody. Ground support had pushed into the spot just as Kotler and Denzel managed to swing over the edge of the rock. They'd made short work of ending the skirmish after the helicopters had taken out most of the enemy.

Kotler and Denzel were treated for minor abrasions and injuries and were deemed fit to release.

They met with some of the Egyptian military personnel, who were more than happy to brief them on everything that had transpired, including the condition of Martook Maalyck.

"He is alive," one man, the Ra'id in charge, told them. "His condition is critical, but he is being cared for. He will be transported to Cairo when he is well enough."

Kotler was relieved to hear it. He smiled as he looked around. Sarraf's men were being loaded into one of the transports, and Kotler noted that at least one face didn't seem to be among them. "What about Dr. Nesahor? Was he killed during the fight?"

The Ra'id shook his head, confused. "Dr. Nesahor was here? We had no word of this."

Kotler exchanged a look with Denzel. He turned back to the Ra'id. "Was there another vehicle here? Besides the two transports?"

"Satellites only showed us the transports, but we were not looking for other vehicles. We saw nothing on our approach."

Kotler shook his head. "Then he must have left on foot."

"What are the odds he could survive out here, without food or transportation?" Denzel asked.

The Ra'id shrugged. "Not high. The nearest village is the one near the dig site. He would be on his own here."

Kotler turned and scanned the mountains to the horizon. It was formidable terrain. He'd experienced a small part of it himself, during his escape from Ammon, and he knew how harrowing a journey through these mountains could be. Nesahor, if he was out there, might not survive.

But then again ...

"We can't worry about him now," Denzel said. "We have enough to deal with. I'm sure the Egyptian military is going to want us to debrief them." He looked to the Ra'id, who nodded in affirmation.

"What about the artifacts?" Kotler asked. "They ... they weren't in that truck, were they?" He motioned to the cliff's edge.

"We have recovered them from the equipment transport," the Ra'id said.

Kotler nodded. "Good. I have a feeling there are more secrets for that sword to unlock."

"Perhaps later," the Ra'id said. "Now, if you will come with me."

He led them to one of the helicopters, where Kotler and

Denzel strapped in. Moments later they lifted off and glided above the mountains, and half an hour later they had covered the terrain it had taken two hours to cover in the trucks. They landed at the camp, which was now being used as a base of operations for the military. And as they exited the helicopter, they were guided to Sarraf's former trailer. They were made comfortable, given food and water and coffee, and told to settle in.

They were going to be there for a while.

Two DAYS later Kotler and Denzel were finally cleared, even encouraged, to return to the United States.

"The Egyptian government thanks you for your assistance," they were told. "But your presence here is no longer required."

It wasn't exactly an order to leave the country, but it was clear that the Egyptians would prefer they moved on. There was the impression that they blamed Kotler and Denzel for what had gone down here, though they'd been made aware of the Alihat Iadida, and of both Sarraf's and Nesahor's involvement with the cult.

That awareness may have been all that prevented Kotler and Denzel from being loaded onto a plane at gunpoint and banned from ever returning.

As Kotler and Denzel walked through the camp on what was sure to be their final day, Denzel said, "I'm sorry Kotler. I know you were excited about doing some work here."

Kotler considered this, looking around at the site as they passed tents and people resuming their duties. He recognized many of the archaeologists, most of whom he had worked with on various digs in the past. The work had been disrupted here, but it would start again. That was how things went, at a site such as this one.

He smiled and shook his head. "It's ok. I think I've had my fill of this place. My only regret is that I didn't get a chance to see what was on the other side of that stone. The Otherworld site."

"Will they send anyone in there?" Denzel asked.

Kotler nodded. "Eventually. There's a military presence there now, guarding it to make sure Nesahor or some other member of the Alihat Iadida doesn't return. I'm out of the loop now, so I have no idea what the Egyptian government intends to do there. "

"Maybe they'll invite you back," Denzel offered. "This whole thing wasn't your fault, after all."

"Maybe," Kotler shrugged. He felt a little bittersweet about the whole thing. He was still recovering from his own trek through mountains, just three days earlier, though his strength had returned in full. But there were other injuries. Seeing Martook stabbed in front of him. Knowing how close Denzel had come to being killed himself. These things tainted his sense of curiosity about the site. He found he just wanted to leave it to someone else, to move on.

It wasn't that returning to this site had been a mistake. It had simply changed Kotler's experience with the place. For twenty years he'd occasionally remembered his adventure with Martook, discovering the brass hall and recovering Credne's sword. He'd had some regret—that he'd been forced to leave the site he'd uncovered. But coming back here had provided some closure. Maybe not on all fronts, but in the ways that mattered. He could leave the rest for someone else, knowing he'd done all he could to make further exploration possible.

They came to the tent that had been their destination—the medical triage where several people now occupied beds. Maalyck was among them.

He had made a good recovery, though he was still too critical to transport out. He was awake, however, and lucid. He saw Kotler and Denzel as they entered, and he gestured for them to come closer.

He had a computer on his lap, and he closed it and placed it on a small table beside his bed, wincing slightly from the movement. He gently swept a hand through the lines of IV tubes and monitor wires, disentangling them and letting them drop down beside his bed. "Dr. Kotler," he smiled. "I have wonderful news!"

"Shouldn't you be resting?" Kotler smiled back, gesturing toward the laptop. "All of this can wait until you've been released from the hospital."

Maalyck shook his head, and winced from the motion, but continued to smile. "I am fine. I will be fine. But I have been in communication with my people at the museum. And they have been in touch with the government. I have convinced them!"

Kotler shook his head. "Convinced them of what?"

"I have convinced them to let you be the one to enter the Otherworld chamber! You will be the one who uncovers its secrets, for the benefit of the world!"

Kotler exchanged a look with Denzel, who looked as bemused as Kotler felt. "Martook ... Roland and I have been asked to leave Egypt. Today."

"Old news," Maalyck said, waving a dismissive hand. "My news is new. The military here hasn't been caught up yet. They will receive new orders within the hour. And you were never asked to leave. I'm told it was merely ... suggested. But you are still the museum's first choice to lead the research here."

Kotler shook his head and laughed. "I ... I don't know what to say. I'm honored that they still have that kind of faith in me."

"They know that you were not the cause of any of this," Maalyck said. He looked at Denzel then. "They know as well that it was Nesahor and Sarraf who stole the artifacts from this camp." He paused and continued in a stern voice. "With no help from anyone else."

Denzel's eyebrows went up, and he smiled. "Oh do they? That explains the complete lack of questions about those artifacts when we were being debriefed."

Maalyck grinned. "The moment I learned of Nesahor's involvement, I told them all about it."

Kotler shook his head and chuckled. "So it looks like I'm sticking around for a bit. But ..." he looked at Denzel. "What about you?" Kotler turned back to Maalyck. "Do I have any leeway in choosing my team? For opening that chamber?"

Maalyck nodded. "I thought you might want such latitude. I have made arrangements. Agent Denzel is free to accompany you if you wish."

Kotler looked back to Denzel, questioning.

Denzel shook his head and laughed. "How could I refuse?"

Kotler grinned and asked Maalyck, "When can we leave?"

CHAPTER TWENTY-EIGHT

THE OTHERWORLD SITE looked very different with an official Egyptian military presence. Several tents and trailers had been erected, and a fence had been set up around the perimeter, encasing the entire plateau. Armed men were stationed in posts around the camp at strategic spots, eliminating any chance that anyone could approach without being seen. Kotler and Denzel were the only non-military people onsite.

Kotler had opted to keep his team light. He had permission to enter the chamber below but had also been advised that any other personnel would have to endure a two-day background check. As Denzel had already had such a check, as part of their debriefing, he could accompany Kotler. Bringing anyone else from the Credne site would cause delays.

"We'll document everything," Kotler said. "And we can hand it off to someone else, once we have a bead on what's down there."

"Who would you hand it off too?" Denzel asked. "Dr. Maalyck?"

Kotler nodded. "He'd be my very first choice if he wants it.

It's going to take time for him to recover, but I don't think anyone will mind the delay. It will give the museum and the government time to vet anyone Martook chooses to be on the team."

They were standing at the edge of the ravine now, looking down at the shelf below. Unlike Kotler's first trip down the side of this cliff, this time he would be lowered on a platform, along with any equipment he needed. He was inspecting the equipment now.

On the whole, Kotler kept things simple and light, confining everything to tow climber's packs.

Lights would be crucial, as would a few small tools. Along with flashlights and clip-on lights, each pack included a couple of small diffused light kits that could be set up anywhere.

Each pack also contained radios to communicate with the surface, though the further they went into the mountain the less useful these would be.

The rest of the gear consisted of ropes and other climbing equipment, as well as a camera and a few tools and instruments they would use to document what they found.

Kotler watched as Denzel shoved energy bars and other food into his pack.

Denzel looked up at him and shrugged. "Old habits. Eat and sleep when you can, because you never know when you're going to go without for a while."

Kotler chuckled, and then, thinking about it, shoved a few energy bars into his own pack and made sure his water bottle was full.

Once preparations were made, Kotler discussed their plans with the military personnel on site, giving them a timeline for their expected return. There was no way to know how deep they'd have to go, or what they'd encounter along the way, but he estimated they should be back up top in about twelve hours.

"It's likely that once we're inside the mountain, we won't have much radio contact. The stone will block the signal. But when I can, I'll check in."

"We will be here," the Ra'id said, nodding.

Kotler and Denzel stepped onto the platform then, packs at their feet, and were lowered to the rock shelf by a crane.

As the platform settled to the ledge, the two of them disembarked and set to inspecting the entryway. The platform would remain, tethered to a piton driven into the rock face. There was a control panel on the platform that would allow Kotler and Denzel to activate the crane and lift themselves out, should they need it.

As they looked over the entry, Kotler brushed away small chips of stone and pushed against the remaining rock to gauge its stability.

When the truck had fallen on it, the impact had fractured the stone, splitting it at an angle. Large chunks of the rock had broken away and fallen with the truck, creating a gap at the top that was wide enough for Kotler and Denzel to squeeze through. Kotler went in first, and Denzel handed their packs through to him one at a time, then followed.

Inside, Kotler turned on a flashlight, and Denzel did the same. They would move cautiously, with Kotler in the lead, inspecting the path before them for any signs of a trap or other dangers.

"How are you doing so far?" Kotler asked.

Denzel had gone quiet and a bit pale as they'd entered the tunnel, but he nodded. "I'm fine. Managing. I've had enough experiences in tight space lately that it's not bothering me as much."

Kotler studied him, mostly to see if his friend was lying. Denzel seemed stressed, but not so much that he was on the verge of a panic attack. In the three years they'd known each other, Kotler had watched as his friend made terrific strides in overcoming his claustrophobia. Primarily as a result of being forced to deal with it again and again.

As if reading Kotler's mind, Denzel said, "We sure end up in a lot of caves and underground tunnels."

Kotler chuckled. "At least we're not being chased by armed mercenaries this time."

Denzel nodded his agreement, and the two of them moved deeper into the mountain.

Progress was slow but steady. Kotler was being cautious, unsure if there might be dangers hidden here. This area seemed far more geologically stable than the Credne site, so that was one worry off his mind. There hadn't been any sort of traps embedded in the other chambers, but this was different. The Otherworld was, according to Druidic mythology, the domain of the gods. If this site was meant to be that, or even just a gateway to it, the builders might have wanted to protect it.

Of course, placing it in a cave accessible only to those brave or insane enough to make the climb might have seemed like sufficient protection. But there was no harm in being cautious.

And it was his caution that alerted him to certain anomalies.

"Huh," Kotler said, stopping and kneeling to inspect the stone walkway.

"What is it?" Denzel asked.

Kotler shook his head. "This path was carved by the builders, thousands of years ago. It must have been a massive effort, cutting into the stone to flatten and level this surface. They didn't do this in any of the other chambers, except perhaps the brass hall. It makes sense that they'd put more effort into this place." He motioned to the walls, which were natural stone, but bore carvings of runes and symbols, woven patterns that were meant as wards against intruders with ill intent, and as prayers to the gods to which this path led. "From what I can tell, this place was sealed a millennium ago, at the same time as the other chambers. But looking at the dust on this path, it looks ... disturbed."

"As in someone has been in here?" Denzel asked, suddenly on alert. "Recently?"

Kotler looked up and nodded. "It's difficult to tell. There really isn't much dust. It could just be a coincidence."

"How many legitimate coincidences have you experienced in the past few years?" Denzel asked.

Kotler shook his head. His partner was right, and just the fact that Kotler sensed something amiss was enough reason to be on guard. "You didn't happen to bring a gun, did you?" he asked.

Denzel huffed. "Kotler, I'm on vacation. We don't get to bring our guns to foreign countries when we're on vacation. Did you see me put a gun in my pack?"

"Just asking," Kotler said, getting to his feet. He shrugged his pack off of his shoulders and patted a side pocket, removing the multi-tool he'd stored there. "I never got to use this, before," he said, holding it up for Denzel to see. "I kind of think of it as a good luck charm now." He slipped the tool into his pants pocket, keeping it within reach.

"Maybe I should have kept that satellite phone," Denzel grumbled. He placed his own pack on the ground and pulled out a small climbing hammer, its head angled sharply. He hefted it, satisfied. "Just in case." He slipped the hammer into his belt.

"Just in case," Kotler agreed, hoping they were being paranoid.

They pressed on, and as they walked the carvings in the tunnel walls were soon accompanied by statues and other objects. Most were made of local stone. Some were made of jade and other imported materials. Finally, they began to see brass, silver, gold.

The walls here contained intaglios of fine gold thread, laid to illustrate vignettes of ancient battles and summits between beings of high power.

Kotler stopped, stunned.

"This ... this is incredible," he whispered.

Denzel stood beside him, examining a wall etched with a scene of several figures standing over a battlefield. The soldiers were at ease, bearing pikes and swords and shields, standing ready on the battle line. Pennants appeared to wave in a breeze long stilled by time. Bodies of fallen soldiers littered the grounds, but the survivors stood, watching. This was a battle that had been halted in mid-fight, while men and women of authority parlayed on the field.

"The gods," Kotler said, his voice filled with awe.

"The Druid folks?" Denzel replied. "Credne and the others? The ... the Toothy Dannans?"

"Tuatha dé Danann," Kotler corrected. "And yes. But not just the Tuatha dé. Look here. That's ... I think that's Thor. See the hammer? It's shaped like the Norse depictions of it. And there, that one-eyed man would be Odin. But more remarkable, look here. That man holding a bolt of lightning ... Zeus. And here, this woman with eight arms. I think that's Durga, from the Hindu pantheon. And this figure with an elephant's head is Ganesha." He was moving now, leaning closer to inspect the figures. There were hundreds of them, each finely detailed with inlaid gold. "Here!" Kotler said. "This figure with the head of a jackal. That's Anubis. This one, with a falcon's head. Horus. There is Ra, Sekhmet, Isis. Egyptian gods." He turned away finally, his face flushed. "Roland ... there are gods here from every known pantheon, from around the world. Including a few I don't even recognize!"

He turned back to the scene, studying it with giddy delight.

Denzel moved to a new position, examining it himself. "Kotler," he said, his voice quiet but firm. "I recognize this one."

Kotler pulled away reluctantly, joining Denzel to study the wall from his vantage point. Kotler spotted a number of recognizable gods in the display but froze when he saw what Denzel was looking at.

Before them was a humanoid figure bearing the head of an owl. The owl's head was composed of a series of circles, and it appeared to be turning its head to the side as if observing the scene before it quizzically.

From the right perspective, the owl's face could appear to be a large and exaggerated skull.

"Isn't that ..." Denzel hesitated, thinking. "That's ... that's Ah-choo."

"Ah-Puch," Kotler said quietly. He reached out a hand to trace the gold filament that formed the shape of the Mayan god of death.

"My God," Kotler said.

They had encountered paintings and statues of Ah-Puch while investigating the murder of Maggie Hamilton, the Broadway star whose body had been discovered in a Mayan tomb. The name, Ah-Puch, had also been used for a biological weapon that could have been used to devastating effect. Kotler and Denzel had managed to stop it from being used for nefarious purposes and had helped in solving Maggie's disappearance and murder.

Ah-Puch was a bit hard to forget.

But here, thousands of miles from Central America, he was in a place where he simply did not belong.

"How did they know about this guy?" Denzel asked.

Kotler shook his head. "I don't know. It's ... it's impossible."

He looked at the surrounding figures and was astonished to

see dozens that he recognized from the Mayan and Aztec pantheons. Quetzalcoatl, Viracocha, Kukulkan. It was a whos-who of American gods, none of whom belonged on a wall in Egypt, thousands of years before the Americas were even discovered.

Kotler had to make himself breathe. "It means that there really was a link between these cultures. These gods ... they somehow knew and interacted with each other. This scene is from the conclusion of a battle. A summit of the gods, to bring peace." Kotler shook his head again, then returned to his pack, retrieving a camera. He busied himself with documenting the wall, getting the details as well as wider shots, for context. He had Denzel hold the lights, to help bring out the details.

After half an hour Kotler felt he'd captured as much of the mural as he could. There was still more to explore. "I'm just blown away," he said, unable to be much more articulate on the subject.

"Same here," Denzel replied, and Kotler looked to see if his friend might be teasing him. But the expression on Denzel's face said a lot. The agent was no fool. He knew what this would mean for history as they knew it. Proof that ancient cultures knew of each other and interacted with each other. Evidence of an earlier civilization, advanced beyond anything modern archaeology had imagined. This was world-changing in its implications.

"We'd better get going," Denzel said. "We're eating into our timeline. There's bound to be more to find."

Kotler laughed. "Now you're sounding like an archaeologist," he said. They packed up and moved along, deeper into the path to the Otherworld.

CHAPTER TWENTY-NINE

Past the mural, around a bend in the path, the entire space opened into a wider chamber, about the size of a hotel lobby. The chamber was clearly hand-hewn, carved with ornate figures, runes, and more vignettes. Kotler was taken immediately by a statue depicting Danu, also known as Dana—the Celtic goddess who was the oldest and most beautiful among the Druidic pantheon, and the source of their name: *Tuatha dé Danann.*

The people of Dana.

Kotler stood straight, inspecting the room, suddenly realizing where they stood.

"This is it," he said to Denzel. "The Otherworld."

"Seems small," Denzel said.

Kotler shook his head. "It's bigger than it looks. This is just an antechamber." He looked around and spotted what he was after. "There," he said, pointing.

Denzel followed his gesture. Across the space, beyond the statuary and carvings, was an arch of stone mostly hidden from view by a screen composed of three large, golden panels. The beams of their flashlights played over the gold intaglio, highlighting its details.

"See the motif? The treeing within a circle of its own branches? That's the Celtic tree of life. And it's etched across three panels."

"Three," Denzel said. "You said three was an important number to the Druids. It's a hint, right? Three deities?"

"Exactly," Kotler replied, grinning. "The inlay itself also hints at something important. The tree of life, in this depiction, is a grand oak. That's significant. Oak, ash, birch. These three, in particular, had great significance in Druidic practices. The name itself, 'druid,' is a derivation. The Celtic word for oak tree is 'Duir.' Combined with the Indo-European word for knowledge, 'wid,' we get 'Duir-wid.' Or 'one with knowledge of the oak.' Over time, as many phrases do, it became simply 'Druid.'"

He looked up to see Denzel studying the intaglio, nodding along. For once Kotler's partner wasn't annoyed with his proclivity for sharing the minutia of history. Emboldened, Kotler continued.

"This inlay is important for another reason, particular to its placement here," he said. "The Druids believed that trees provided tethers between the Otherworld and Earth. Those panels represent a gateway."

"Kotler, are you telling me that on the other side of those panels is some kind of magic portal to another world?"

Kotler chuckled. "Magic? I can't say. The world is full of mysteries, so I can't exactly discount the idea. But I can say that there's a good chance we're going to find something pretty amazing on the other side of that screen."

Denzel considered that. "Ok," he said. "So what do we do?"

"We go investigate," Kotler grinned.

Standing before the panels, just inches from them, Kotler was taken by their immense size. Rising from the floor to the ceiling, they were perhaps ten feet tall, and each was about four feet wide. Kotler leaned in, shining his flashlight over the details of the screens, illuminating the twists and turns of the roots and branches of the tree of life. Each ultimately curved to meet the other, indicating the circular nature of existence, and the relationship between life and the afterlife, in Druidic culture.

Kotler ran his fingers over the seams between the screens.

"That's ... unexpected," he said.

"What is it?" Denzel asked, leaning in to see for himself.

"I think ... it looks like there are no locks or other means to secure these. I can't find any latches. They look as if we could just push them open."

"So, what, they're just waiting for you to open them? What does that mean?"

Kotler shook his head. He wasn't sure what it meant. Perhaps the builders of this place had decided that anyone who found it would be worthy. It seemed unfathomable, after all the elaborate mechanisms and security measures found at the Credne site. But as Kotler inspected the panels, he found nothing to indicate that he and Denzel, or anyone else, would be barred from entering.

He reached out and pushed the center panel.

It moved, slowly but with some minor resistance, similar to pushing on a spring-hinged door. And as Kotler looked at the widening seam, he realized that was precisely what this was. Shining his light into the gap, he could see layered strips of brass, bulging and flexing with the movement of the door, like the suspension of an old truck bed. These were ancient leaf springs—technology that no culture should have even imagined prior to the eighteenth century. He had Denzel move the panel while Kotler shot video of the springs in action.

The astounding finds were piling up at this site, while the

THE GOD EXTINCTION 209

assumptions about history and technology and human development were starting to fall by the wayside.

Kotler passed the beam of his flashlight into the space beyond the screen and saw that a path curved out of sight ahead.

"It's symbolic," he smiled.

"Symbolic?" Denzel asked.

Kotler looks up at him. "The screen. It's a tether. The tree of life. A gateway to the Otherworld. Passing through this means we're there. We're entering the realm of the Tuatha dé Danann. The realm of the gods."

"And we're sure there are no acid gods or pointing spike gods or some other nasty thing waiting for us to walk through there?" Denzel asked.

Kotler laughed. "There may be, but I don't think so. It's the tree of life, not the tree of acid burns and impalement." He swept his flashlight beam over the room around them. "Look at this place. There was some event that inspired this. It was a time of peace, among the gods and their peoples. Maybe a peace brokered in war, but from what I'm seeing they came to some sort of agreement. A truce, perhaps. I think this place is a memorial to it."

"So you think it should be fine to pass through here," Denzel said.

"I do," Kotler nodded. "You game?"

"Ready when you are," Denzel replied, cinching the straps of his pack a bit tighter.

Kotler smiled, and led the way, passing through the gap in the screens and into the curving corridor beyond.

They walked for only a few moments before the path took a series of sharp turns, veering at right angles to their left and then their right, and then opening wider than either of them had expected. The stone of the mountain fell away around them, and the air and energy, even the sound, suddenly changed. Kotler felt an ionic charge on his skin, and the exhilaration of fresh oxygen hitting his longs.

They shut off their flashlights. There was no need for them. The chamber ahead of them was filled with light.

"What the hell ..." Denzel said quietly, reverently.

Kotler shook his head, unable to even speak, his mind struggling to make sense of the vastness, the impossibility, of what lay in front of him.

The scene before them was a valley, stretching off into a horizon that was nearly invisible, not merely for its great distance but for the foliage and growth that obscured their view.

Before them was a valley of lush and vibrant green.

Kotler looked up to the ceiling and could just make out a dotted landscape of bright spots of light, as if the stars had suddenly come closer to the Earth, filling the canopy of the sky with increased brightness. A thousand small suns, bringing daylight into the depths of the mountain, feeding the life here with their light and their warmth.

"Quartz," Kotler said. It felt like a whisper, though he'd said it aloud. The sound here was white noise, quiet but filling the space, eliminating any hint of echo or reverberation. He hadn't quite worked out what it was, he was so distracted by the presence of light. "Quartz portals," he continued. "Like those we found at the Credne site, and at the brass hall. My God, look at it!"

"Look at all of it," Denzel said, marveling. He was turning slowly, taking in the view of the underground forest. "How can this stuff be growing down here? That's ... are those oak trees?"

Kotler, startled, looked closer at the trees for the first time. Denzel was right. Near them was a standing oak, rising high into the vaulted chamber, its branches spread wide.

It wasn't the only anomalous tree. From what Kotler could see there were stands of birch and ash, as well as a few varieties he didn't recognize. And among them were plants that did not belong in this region—brush and vines that were more at home in the ranges of Ireland than here in the deserts of Egypt.

"There must be some underground water source," Kotler said. He listened for a moment. "Can you hear that? It sounds like ... maybe rapids? A waterfall?"

"I hear it," Denzel said. "I'm just not sure I believe it." He looked at Kotler, a smile plastered on his face. "This is it, isn't it? This is the Otherworld."

"A literal place," Kotler grinned, shaking his head. "It's just unbelievable."

"Believe it," a man's voice said from the tree line.

Kotler and Denzel turned, startled, and then slowly raised their hands.

From the impossible forest before them, two figures emerged, each wielding sidearms. One of the figures was an Egyptian soldier—one of Sarraf's men who must have escaped the firefight above.

No, Kotler realized. He looked and saw that the man had been the second solider on the rock shelf. The one who had leapt out into the ravine as the truck fell. His rope must have saved him.

Kotler also recognized the second man.

"Nesahor," Kotler said.

"It is good to see you again, Dr. Kotler," Nesahor said. "Welcome to the Otherworld."

CHAPTER THIRTY

Kotler and Denzel were forced to kneel with their hands behind their heads as the soldier relieved them of their packs. He rifled through these and was delighted to discover the energy bars and water bottles. He delivered these to Nesahor, and the two of them began eating ravenously.

"It's remarkable, isn't it?" Nesahor said, chewing on a bite of an energy bar and indicating the underground valley with a wave. He finished chewing and swallowing before he continued. "Not quite what the Alihat Iadida were expecting, I will confess. There is still much to explore here, but thus far I have found no sign of gods or items of power. Still, the site itself represents quite a find."

"And nothing that would benefit your organization," Kotler said. "The Egyptian military will never allow you to claim this site."

Nesahor shook his head. "Sadly, no. You are correct. But there are other sites. Other paths to take. This one had great promise, but we can accept that it may be lost to us. For now. You would be surprised how easy it is to gain a foothold in even the Egyptian government. Over time, I am certain that we can regain access to this place if we deem it necessary."

"So what now?" Denzel asked. "Kill us?"

Nesahor laughed. "Certainly not. Not unless you force me to. I intend to trade you."

"Trade us?" Kotler asked. "For what?"

"For our freedom, of course," Nesahor said. "You are hostages."

Kotler laughed. "I think you overestimate the value the Egyptian government places on us," he said.

"On you, perhaps," Nesahor nodded. "But Agent Denzel is another matter. They will want to avoid an international incident. So he is our hostage. You ..." Nesahor considered Kotler. "You are leverage."

"You got a problem then," Denzel said. "Neither the Egyptian government nor the US government negotiates with terrorists."

Nesahor laughed. "Terrorists? Please, Agent Denzel. At worst we are thieves. At any rate, I am confident the authorities will grant my request for a vehicle, thinking they'll simply track my movements via satellite."

"But you have another way out, don't you?" Kotler asked.

"Of course," Nesahor said. "I made arrangements before entering the Otherworld."

Kotler turned to the soldier, who was happily munching his second energy bar. He hadn't spoken once since they'd been captured. Thinking back on his previous encounter with the man, Kotler realized the only time the soldier had spoken in his presence, he hadn't used English. It was possible he couldn't even speak the language.

In Arabic, Kotler said, *"And what of you? What do you believe Nesahor will do with you, when we get to the surface? He has made arrangements. And he plans to offer us in trade for his freedom. You are Egyptian military ... do you believe they'll allow you to simply leave, after what you have done?"*

The soldier stopped in mid-chew, considering. He turned to Nesahor, a realization dawning on him. He drew his weapon.

Nesahor, his sidearm already out and at the ready, turned and aimed reflexively at the solider.

Kotler and Denzel both moved, each knowing the other would pick up on the situation and their options.

They sprang, each tackling the man closest to them even as the soldier's sidearm was fired. The sound of the gunshot was loud but died almost immediately in the white noise of the forest valley.

Kotler was on top of the soldier, wrestling him to the ground, punching him while pressing his gun hand to the soil. The man regained some of his composure and fought back with notable effort. Kotler concentrated on getting him to release the pistol, slamming his hand against the packed soil and stone of the valley floor.

Suddenly there was another shot fired, close enough to be startling, and Kotler and the solider both froze in mid-struggle.

"Get up," Denzel's voice said from over Kotler's shoulder.

Kotler turned his head to see his friend standing with Nesahor's gun trained in their general direction. Kotler relieved the soldier of his weapon and climbed to his feet.

The soldier had his hands raised above his head and slowly rose from the ground. Denzel motioned for him to move to where Nesahor was kneeling, and to join the doctor on that spot.

"You should *not* have eaten my energy bars, pal."

Kotler tucked the soldier's pistol into his belt, retrieved their packs, and found a roll of bright orange Paracord inside. He fished the multi-tool out of his pocket, and cut lengths of the cord, then tied each man's hands behind him as Denzel covered him.

Secretly Kotler was relieved that he'd finally gotten to use the multi-tool. He folded it closed, bounced it in his palm, and then tucked it back into his pocket.

Once the work of securing their prisoners was done, Denzel relaxed and lowered his weapon.

Kotler stood in front of Nesahor, looking down on the man. Nesahor met his gaze, contempt plain on his face.

"I know a bit about your background," Kotler said. "I read up on you, before leaving camp to come here. I was curious about your history, about how you might have gotten involved with the Alihat Iadida. You have a long and lettered history. Papers published in some of the most prestigious journals in the world. You've done so much good in this field, helped solve so many riddles. What is it about the Alihat Iadida that would make you throw away all of your credibility, all of your accomplishments?"

Nesahor laughed. "Accomplishments? We have been scratching in the dirt for hundreds of years, Dr. Kotler, and we have barely begun to uncover our real heritage. But there is something that lies under the gilded surface of history. The gods were real. Whether they were beings of mystical power or an advanced race of humans, I cannot say. But I have seen their footprints with my own eyes. I have felt their presence, just at the edge of our awareness. Their extinction from this world left a void. One that the Alihat Iadida—the New Gods—will fill."

"Power, then," Kotler said.

"Power. Life eternal. And the answers that you, yourself, seek. Isn't that right, Dr. Kotler?"

Kotler studied Nesahor and saw that instead of madness or even religious zeal, there was something else driving him. The man was filled with something more profound than greed or avarice. Something that went beyond merely a quest for power.

Nesahor truly believed in the gods. And more, he truly believed he had the right to be one of them.

Kotler shook his head, saying nothing. He and Denzel chatted quietly while watching the two men, ensuring neither of them tried to escape. As they discussed options, it became obvious that they would have to leave this place. And given the situation here, and the revelations they had already uncovered, it was possible the Egyptian government would clamp down on the site until it could be properly explored by a well-vetted team.

This might be the last time Kotler ever got to see the place.

He shot video and photos, narrated some of his observations, made notes of everything that occurred to him. He immersed himself in this while Denzel made preparations to take their two prisoners out and back to the surface, where they would be handed off to the Egyptian military.

After a while Kotler resigned himself to tucking everything away, replacing the camera equipment and pulling his pack over his shoulders. He joined Denzel, who had the two men standing in front of him, facing the stone archway that led back to the antechamber. They would make rapid progress, going out. They wouldn't stop to investigate anything, as they had on the way in. This was the end of the excursion.

"You good?" Denzel asked.

Kotler chuckled. "Just taking it in. This place," he shook his head and looked around. "There's so much I could explore here. So many questions I might be able to answer. And it's just ... it's not going to be my work."

Denzel watched him for a moment and nodded. "You might be invited back."

"Maybe," Kotler smiled. But he didn't believe it. This site, and all of its wonders, would be explored and studied by someone else. Its secrets might not even be revealed to the world for years, even decades. Depending on what was found here, and the sensitivity it inspired in the Egyptian authorities, Kotler might never learn anything of it.

Someone else would have to pick up the gauntlet thrown down by this place and look into the deepening mystery of what it meant for the shared culture of humanity. Perhaps that person would be Maalyck.

Kotler hoped that it would.

They left the forest behind, each of them pushing one of the other men ahead of them. Within the hour they were close enough to the exit to reach the base camp by radio. Shortly after that, they were topside, and following a debriefing, they were escorted to a transport. As Kotler had figured, the site would be sealed until further notice.

As they rode away from the site in one of the military Jeeps, Kotler looked back, taking it in one last time, remembering the impossible forest beneath the stone of this plateau. He sighed and turned back to face the rough terrain ahead.

The gods, whoever they had been, might be extinct, but they were not finished revealing their secrets. Not just yet.

Answers, he decided, would one day come.

EPILOGUE

Central Park, New York

LUDLUM HAD to admit that the whole scenario felt like something out of a thriller novel. She had followed instructions, had arrived at the park and made her way to the bridge. This part of Central Park was somewhat isolated, though it was also somewhat famous. This area, and the very bridge she was approaching, had been a part of a number of films set in New York. The isolation lent itself to a bit of romance and intrigue.

And there were many scenes portraying this exact scenario —a clandestine meeting, arranged by an unseen and unknown figure, claiming to know what she was up to. Claiming to have information she would want.

Ludlum spotted the flower in the man's lapel. The sign she'd been told to look for. She approached.

"Dr. Ludlum," the man said. He was older, perhaps in his seventies or early eighties. His hair was steel grey and swept under the brim of a dark gray fedora. He was even wearing the black pea coat. Every inch a spy, by her estimate. Or someone living out a fantasy, which seemed far more likely.

"Who are you?" Ludlum asked.

He smiled and shook his head. "You know, of course, I have no intention of telling you. But I've become aware of what you and Agent Brown are doing. Looking into the charter for Historic Crimes."

Ludlum felt her heart pounding, but she kept her breathing steady. She'd gotten a text message with instructions to be here, at this time, and to meet this man. It had outlined some of what she'd done so far, in her research into Historic Crimes. She'd been told to come here if she wanted more answers. She'd been told to tell no one.

But of course, she'd told Dani immediately. Agent Brown wasn't far away, sitting at a bench within sprinting distance of this spot. She was listening via Ludlum's phone, which was tucked into the chest pocket of her coat. It was the best they could manage on short notice, without raising suspicion at the FBI, with a surveillance request.

Ludlum was also armed, her FBI-issued sidearm in a holster inside her coat. She was taking a risk by being here, but she'd be insane to go in unarmed.

"Are you here to tell me to stop?" Ludlum asked the man.

Again he smiled and laughed lightly. "No. I'm here to tell you to keep going. But to be more careful." He reached into his coat and pulled something small out of his pocket. He reached toward her, and she instinctively lifted her hand to receive it.

The man placed a small object in Ludlum's palm. A thumb drive. "This will help. But use it on an air-gapped computer."

He turned to leave, and Ludlum caught up with him. "Wait," she said. "I need to know what's going on. If you won't tell me who you are, will you at least tell me why you're helping? How did you know what I was looking into? How do I know you're not setting me up for something?"

The man shook his head. "If I were setting you up, would I have continued to talk to you even though you brought Agent Brown along?" He grinned. "Of the two of us, I'm the one showing the most trust, don't you think?"

"How did you ..."

"You're not the only one with friends, Dr. Ludlum." He glanced around at the trees and stones of the park, and Ludlum followed his gaze.

They were more or less alone here, but not far from this spot people were milling about, walking and chatting, sitting and observing. Any one of them, Ludlum realized, could be there to watch them.

"I can tell you that this is about Dr. Kotler," the man said. "All of it."

Ludlum shook her head. "You're ... wait, you're saying not just this, but ... Historic Crimes? The department itself?"

"All of it," the man repeated. "Be careful, going forward. Both of you. There are aspects of this that someone doesn't want discovered. Isn't that just the way?" He chuckled. "I'm leaving. Don't follow me. Go back to Agent Brown, and the two of you go find a computer you can use to look those over." He nodded to her palm, and Ludlum self-consciously slipped the thumb drive into her coat pocket.

She stood and watched the man walk away, but before he got too far, she asked, "How can I reach you? If we need to ask questions?"

"I'll be in touch," the man said without looking back. Ludlum watched as he walked into the tunnel under the bridge and disappeared after leaving the far end.

She wandered back to Dani, dropping down beside her on

the bench. The agent was frowning. "What the hell is going on?" she asked.

Ludlum shook her head and sat in silence, thinking.

She wasn't sure what they should do next. But she did know one thing for certain. "We can't tell Dan about this. Or Agent Denzel. Not until we have more."

Dani looked at her, shook her head, and sighed. "Ok," she agreed. "We say nothing. But that guy was right. We have to be more careful. If someone like that has caught wind of what we're doing, then someone else has, too."

Ludlum nodded, then stood. "Let's go. I need to buy a laptop."

They left the park, taking Dani's sedan, merging into the New York City traffic.

Ludlum let her mind wander as Dani drove, thinking over the encounter, over what she'd learned so far. It wasn't much. She had only just gotten started. With Dani passing her information only as she could retrieve it, progress had been pretty slow. Ludlum had started branching out, using some of her NYPD contacts, even chatting with members of the forensics community.

It was slow, tedious work, reverse engineering Historic Crimes, searching for its origins. Whoever created their charter hadn't wanted their name to come up.

What was it, Ludlum wondered, that had gotten this man's attention? What part of her search had taken her too close to whatever this mysterious person in the background wanted to keep hidden?

Careful, Ludlum thought. *Be careful.*

She could be a lot more careful, she thought, if she knew which nerves she was hitting.

For now, she would slow down a little, until she could see and make sense of whatever was on this thumb drive.

But the answers were coming.

A NOTE AT THE END

Sugar Land, Texas

This book is a sequel in more ways than one.

First—and I sincerely hope this comes through naturally and organically—it's another fully-developed volume in the continuing story of Dan Kotler and Roland Denzel. Like the six full-length novels that came before it, this book is meant to expand on the mythos of a character I've come to love writing about. It's meant to be fun, intriguing, even a little informative.

But second, and maybe even more important, this book is a sequel to a story that readers have been asking about since I first starting writing thrillers. This story picks up where *The Brass Hall* left off—albeit twenty years after the events of that tale.

In case you've never read it, *The Brass Hall* is a novella I wrote at the same time I was writing *The Coelho Medallion*, the first full novel in this series. In truth, *Brass Hall* is technically the very first Dan Kotler thriller, released just before the release of the full novel. I wrote it while I was doing edits and revisions on the book, as a way to ease my existing list of sci-fi readers into the idea that I was going to try my hand at a whole new genre.

At that time, I was releasing a lot of novella-length and short-story-length books, experimenting to see if I would enjoy writing more grounded fiction. I was also testing the waters for short fiction, to see if there was a market for it. I believe there is, but I've come to realize it's a slightly different market than that of my full-length novels.

At any rate, *Brass Hall* was always meant as a soft introduction and a prequel to the Dan Kotler series. "Soft," because though it featured Kotler doing heroic deeds as well as dealing with the "misplaced history" that I wanted at the heart of my books, it lacked some of the elements I knew would eventually become staples for the series. Most notably, Agent Roland Denzel was nowhere to be found in the story, and in fact, the FBI itself never gets a mention.

Brass Hall was more of an *Indiana Jones*, pulp-fiction type of tale, where the hero and his sidekick face an ancient mystery and modern dangers, coming out of it all with a MacGuffin—a treasure—and maybe a few scrapes and bruises.

Martook, the young sidekick in the story, has never been directly mentioned in any of the books since that tale. He was a crucial part of the story, and without him, Kotler would never have found himself in that predicament. But I've never explored that character any further. Until now.

Over the years (and it seems odd saying it that way, since both *Brass Hall* and *Coelho Medallion* were released in 2016, and it's only now 2019, as I write this), I've gotten a lot of reviews and emails and private messages on social media, asking when I'll get around to turning *Brass Hall* into a full novel. I've had reviews claiming it was too short, that they wanted more, that they'd gladly buy a book that took that story further.

Those comments and requests nudged me, but I also had questions to consider: Whatever happened to Martook, after his adventure with Kotler? Whatever happened to the Brass Hall? As intriguing as it was to discover a Druidic site hidden in the mountains of Egypt, why has there never been any follow-up? This was potentially earth-shaking news (literally, in the case of Kotler and Martook's escape from the Brass Hall), but it appeared to have no repercussions in Kotler's world.

These questions, and the requests, nagged at me. Not so much that they halted everything for me, but they were always there.

As I wrote five more books in the Dan Kotler series, there were little whispers, always tickling the back of my neck. There were nudges and side-trails. And there was a desire. I wanted to go back, to pick up where *Brass Hall* left off, and to tell the rest of the story. I wanted it as much as readers wanted to see it.

The trouble was, how?

So here was the challenge I faced, and it's more about practicality than anything: I had the novella, *The Brass Hall*, already out in the world, already getting reviews and making sales. If I wanted to expand on the story, what was the best way to handle it?

If I went back to it and picked up literally where it left off, should I release it as the same book, just putting in a note to say it was "new and expanded?" Or should I publish the expanded book as its own volume, and start over with reviews and sales?

If I started over, should I take the original novella off the market?

And what about people who had already read that novella? Could I justify asking them to pony up another five bucks for a book that contained a novella they'd already read? Would they consider that a money-gram or a rip-off? Would I alienate my audience while trying to please them?

See? There was a lot to consider. Decisions like these are never as easy as they appear.

Where I landed on this, initially, was that I would go ahead and include the novella as the first few chapters of the new book—Part I of the novel. I'd give this book a whole new title and then skip ahead to twenty years later, where I could pick up the story from a more familiar Dan Kotler, along with his FBI partner and the history we've learned about them to date. I'd make it clear, maybe in the book description or somewhere else, that this book contained that other story, that you might consider skipping ahead if you'd already read *The Brass Hall*. But otherwise, "welcome to the next Dan Kotler book."

I had decided that some readers wouldn't be happy with this decision and that I would just have to appease them the best I could. Maybe I could offer a free short story to anyone who didn't like having a third of the new book turn out to be content they'd already read. Would that be enough?

I wasn't really sure. But I figured I'd deal with it when the time came.

With that in mind, I dropped the novella into the book and got to work on expanding the story from there.

I got pretty far, too. I wrote in some scenes that I felt would neatly bridge the novella and the modern story. I brought back Martook as Dr. Martook Maalyck, giving him a last name for the first time, and starting to flesh out his backstory to fill in some of the gaps between tales. I decided on the major plot point that would drive all of this, landing on the bronze sword that Kotler and Martook had managed to recover from Credne's hall. I even came up with a title ...

The title ...

Oh, the horror.

Titles are a big deal to me. They are, almost without exception, the very first thing I know about a book going in. I come up with a title, and I write a book to match it. That's been the very best technique for me, over the past decade or so of publishing. I start with the title.

So it has to be right.

This time, things were different. I had a title, but it was kind of coming in after the fact. I had the novella wedged into the story, as its opening chapters, and the title was sort of tacked onto that. And ... well ... it didn't fit. It felt awkward and unnatural. It felt like what it was, in other words—one story masquerading as another.

Weirdly, because the title wasn't "right," it was throwing me off. I found that despite knowing the general direction I wanted to go, I couldn't figure a way to get there. It was like trying to use a map of New Zealand to drive from Iowa to Mississippi. You might make it, eventually, but the map had nothing to do with it.

And that wasn't the only hang-up. There were bigger problems.

With *The Brass Hall* rammed into the book like a whale punched through the hull of a boat, I found I was having a hard time managing the energy and momentum of the thing. It was difficult to impossible to steer.

Unlike previous books in this series, where I would introduce a plot by using a prologue—falling back on the sort of cold open that TV dramas use deftly—I was opening this book with a complete, self-contained story. Beginning, middle, and end. Which meant that there was already a resolution, by the end of Part I of the book. There was no energy or momentum to carry it further.

To reintroduce the mystery and intrigue that would keep the reader turning pages, I wedged a sort of pseudo prologue into place. Scenes very similar to those that open this book were jammed in there. They were different from what you've read here, far less cohesive, and seemingly random when I looked back and considered them in context.

The problem was, I was literally cramming a prologue into the opening of Part II of the book, and it showed. The result felt like a bad anthology, with only two stories. And one of those stories had an opening that wouldn't inspire anyone to turn the page, much less keep reading for 50,000 words.

It made no sense. As a reader, I looked at it and wondered, "Why should I care about this?" As a writer, I looked at it and wondered, "What kind of awkward, pointless mess have I wrought?"

There's an old adage in writing: If it doesn't move the story forward, it doesn't belong. So those scenes had to go.

The trouble was, with those scenes gone I had no natural way to lead the reader into the rest of the book, in a way they'd even remotely care about. I was literally jumping from the end of one completed story to the beginning of another story that might or might not make any sense. Because it was just rambling nonsense.

I can admit that now.

This was a crisis.

Since November 2018 I've been on quite a jag when it comes to writing. I completed *The Antarctic Forgery* and released that in December.

I wrote and released *The Stepping Maze*—perhaps the most complex story I've ever written—by January 25th.

I wrote a new short story, *The Jani Sigil*, to give to readers who joined my mailing list (https://kevintumlinson.com/joinme if you'd like a copy of your own—though eventually, I will have a whole new story to offer there. So hurry!).

And, of course, I started the book you are now reading. Plus all the other things I've written and published, both related and unrelated to my fiction. I estimate that since November 2018

I've written and published a minimum of half a million words. That's a lot for anyone, even a full-time writer.

But suddenly I found myself stymied on a writing project. At least a little.

I was still plugging away on this book, but it had become hard work. Where the previous two books had flowed from me almost like someone else had written them, and I was just typing them up on their behalf, this book was forcing me to fight for it for every inch.

I could tell it wasn't working, and I could tell why. And for about a week, though I kept writing, I didn't know what to do about the way the story was failing.

Until, finally, I realized that I did.

I knew exactly what was wrong.

That novella did not belong in this book.

True, I was writing a sequel—or more accurately, a continuation—of *The Brass Hall*. But that story was done. It had been finished years earlier, had its own readers and fans and detractors. It had its history, and it had run its course. All of the momentum for that story was spent.

So bringing it back now, cramming it into the front end of a new book, was like trying to graft a dead limb onto a young tree. The limb isn't coming back to life, and it's just going to bow the tree into a deformed and sad version of what it could be, never allowing it to grow tall and reach for the skies.

I knew what I had to do.

I pulled the novella out of the book. I retooled the prologue to actually be a prologue. And I gave the book a new title—the title you know it as now—so that I could start telling the story the way it was meant to be told.

This book is a continuation of *The Brass Hall*, there is no doubt. The plot builds on the events of that book, though it's not necessary to have read the novella before reading this novel.

But by casting the dead weight off of it, I was able to make *The God Extinction* into the book it was meant to be.

And I love it.

I love *comparative mythology*. I love the idea that cultures all over the world, even cultures that should have had nothing to do with each other, all share commonalities and themes and even literal connections that can't entirely be explained. The idea of a shared culture, long lost to history, is just about the most intriguing thing I can imagine.

The examples I share on this subject, in the early chapters of this book, are just the beginning for this. I could easily have filled an entire book on the topic, with the research I've uncovered about common mythologies, shared artistic and historical themes, even language and iconology that is literally the same across the cultures. The gods, and their tales, are not unique to one culture. They got around.

I can't say what it means exactly, that so many ancient cultures share commonalities in their mythologies. But I do have theories.

I believe that there was an age of man that is no longer a part of our recorded history. I believe that humanity underwent some great cataclysm, in the mists of our past, that wiped our memory and set us back to a more primitive culture, where we were forced to start again. I believe the gods, as we know them, were remnants of a civilization that knew it was on its way out. They used their technology and wisdom to prepare a new generation as much as possible, leaving marks on ancient, primitive cultures that we are only slowly starting to interpret today.

True?

Maybe. Maybe not.

Intriguing, though. And from my personal research, it feels likely. It's at least cohesive enough that it's driven me to write about it more than once and will probably inspire me to write about it again in the future.

I wanted to explore some of these ideas in this book. I've hinted at it in the past, but I wanted to really get the ball rolling in these pages. I saw, in *The Brass Hall*, an opportunity to start looking closer at this idea, to explore it a bit more.

I've left gaps and holes in it, of course. I've left room for interpretation and for speculation. The Otherworld, as I describe it here, has only revealed a very small part of itself to us. I'm absolutely certain that won't be the last of it. I'll be revisiting this world, someday. Maybe someday soon.

Until then, I have more Kotler stories to explore, more questions to ask, and more riddles to solve. Among those are questions about Kotler himself.

For the past few books, I've introduced what we in the writing biz call a "B-story." I've done this before. If you've read my work from the beginning, the Gail McCarthy storyline was a B-story that ran through several books, until it became the A-story for *The Antarctic Forgery*, where it was finally resolved.

Similarly, I'm now exploring some of Kotler's past, as well as digging in on a few questions that have naturally arisen throughout writing these books. Not the least of which is: Why Historic Crime?

I admit, when I first introduced the idea of a new division of the FBI, aimed at solving history-related crimes, I meant for everyone to take it on faith. I needed an excuse for Kotler and Denzel to continue working together so that I could use their dynamic to help with character development. Lashing them together into a new division of the FBI seemed the best way. It would allow me to bring new challenges to Kotler, in the form of history-related FBI cases that had modern-day and immediate implications.

Sort of an *X-Files* of history.

And it worked. It held up well enough, at least, that no one really seemed to question it. I did have some people point out that the FBI would never waste resources the way it does with this department. Agent Denzel would never have the sort of latitude he has, would never be able to go to the sorts of locations he ends up visiting, in an official capacity. I was asking readers to suspend disbelief, and I make no apologies for it.

But as the series has evolved, I'm finding that it's not enough to merely suspend disbelief. Not long term. If I want to tell the sorts of stories I have in mind for Kotler and Denzel, I'm going to have to pick apart the mythos I've built.

In thinking about that, I realized that I might actually have a story right there in the open. A gold nugget half-buried in the muck of a river bank but peeking through just enough to catch my eye.

These books, after all, have a question at their heart, driving the rest of the story.

"What would happen if Viking remains were discovered in Pueblo, Colorado?"

"What if Atlantis was an island destroyed by a tsunami in the Indian Ocean?"

"What if a lost technology was rediscovered and put to a nefarious use?"

Every one of the Kotler books asks a question like this and then attempts to answer it in a fun and exciting way. So, I wondered, what if I applied that sort of question to the series itself?

The first hint of this was when I questioned the name of the department. After all, "Historic Crimes" technically isn't correct. It should be "Historical Crimes." I had made a goof, early on in the series, but I'd more or less been stuck with it., once the book was published.

In reality, I could have gone back and fixed that, doing a

"find and replace" across those early books, and re-releasing them as new editions. No one would even know or care, by the time the dust settled.

But I thought it would be more fun to call it out, to have Kotler question it since he's such a smart guy. And even more fun to have Denzel tell him to shut up about it.

Now that I'd picked at that thread, though, I started wondering what else I could ask. And so "why Historic Crimes" came up. Also "Why Kotler?" And "Why Denzel?" And "Where does the funding come from?" And "Who founded and championed the division?"

And it grows from there.

Answering these questions will be a B-story throughout the next few books until eventually, everything comes to a head and our heroes have to deal with the story directly. At which point, I'll come up with a new B-story, and we will journey on.

That's part of the fun of this. I have to weave these stories so that they can stand alone, as new readers come into the series. But I also have to make them cohesive, as a growing and expanding universe, with its own rules and its own consequences.

Part of that, ultimately, had to include coming back around to expand on *The Brass Hall*. And though this book isn't exactly as I had planned it to be, I hope you'll agree with me that it's all the better for it. I hope, also, that you agree that this fulfills the sort of unwritten promise of *The Brass Hall*, letting the reader see how it all turned out without rehashing the original story.

In other words, I hope you enjoyed it.

There will be more Dan Kotler thrillers. The character is such a part of me now, I can't imagine not writing in his voice. I'm as excited to see how things turn out as you are, believe me.

Until the next book, take care of yourselves. Keep reading.

234 OF AMILY AT THE END

Keep reaching out. Visit me at kevintumlinson.com, join my mailing list (you get a lot of emails similar to this note, if you like this sort of thing), find more of my books. And just say hello. I respond to emails, and I adore hearing from readers. We have a lot to learn from each other.

God bless,
    Kevin Tumlinson
    Sugar Land, Texas
    February 11, 2019

ALSO BY J. KEVIN TUMLINSON

Dan Kotler

The Coelho Medallion

The Atlantis Riddle

The Devil's Interval

The Girl in the Mayan Tomb

The Antarctic Forgery

The Stepping Maze

The God Extinction

The Spanish Papers

The Hidden Persuaders

The Sleeper's War

The God Resurrection

The Demon Core

Dan Kotler Short Fiction

The Brass Hall - A Dan Kotler Story

The Jani Sigil - FREE short story from BookHip.com/DBXDHP

Dan Kotler Box Sets

The Book of Lost Things: Dan Kotler, Books 1-3

The Book of Betrayals: Dan Kotler, Books 4-6

The Book of Gods and Kings: Dan Kotler, Books 7-9

Quake Runner: Alex Kayne

Shaken

Triggered

Compromised

Aftershock

Historic Crimes Crossovers

The Man Below

The Outsiders Gambit

Evergreen

Evergreen: Book 1

Evergreen: Trace Contact

Citadel

Citadel: First Colony

Citadel: Paths in Darkness

Citadel: Children of Light

Citadel: The Value of War

Colony Girl: A Citadel Universe Story

Sawyer Jackson

Sawyer Jackson and the Long Land

Sawyer Jackson and the Shadow Strait

Sawyer Jackson and the White Room

Think Tank

Karner Blue

Zero Tolerance

Nomad

The Lucid — Co-authored with Nick Thacker

Episode 1

Episode 2

Episode 3

Shorts & Novellas

Getting Gone

Teresa's Monster

The Three Reasons to Avoid Being Punched in the Face

Tin Man

Two Blocks East

Edge

Zero

God Mode

Collections & Anthologies

Citadel: Omnibus

Uncanny Divide — With Nick Thacker & Will Flora

Light Years — The Complete Science Fiction Library

Dead of Winter: A Christmas Anthology — With Nick Thacker, Jim Heskett, David Berens, M.P. MacDougall, R.A. McGee, Dusty Sharp & Steven Moore

YA & Middle Grade

Secret of the Diamond Sword — An Alex Kotler Mystery

Wordslinger (Non-Fiction)

30-Day Author: Develop a Daily Writing Habit and Write Your Book In 30 Days (Or Less)

Watch for more at kevintumlinson.com/books

HERE'S HOW TO HELP ME REACH MORE READERS

If you loved this book, you can help me reach more readers with just a few easy acts of kindness.

(1) REVIEW THIS BOOK

Leaving a review for this book is a great way to help other readers find it. Just go to the site where you bought the book, search for the title, and leave a review. It really helps, and I really appreciate it.

(2) SUBSCRIBE TO MY EMAIL LIST

I regularly write a special email to the people on my list, just keeping everyone up to date on what I'm working on. When I announce new book releases, giveaways, or anything else, the people on my list hear about it first. Sometimes, there are special deals I'll *only* give to my list, so it's worth being a part of the crowd.

Join the conversation and get a free ebook, just for signing up! Visit https://www.kevintumlinson.com/joinme.

(3) TELL YOUR FRIENDS

Word of mouth is still the best marketing there is, so I would greatly appreciate it if you'd tell your friends and family about this book, and the others I've written.

You can find a comprehensive list of all of my books at http://kevintumlinson.com/books.

Thanks so much for your help. And thanks for reading.

ABOUT THE AUTHOR

Kevin Tumlinson is an award-winning and bestselling novelist, living in Texas and working in random coffee shops, cafés, and hotel lobbies worldwide. His debut thriller, *The Coelho Medallion*, was a 2016 Shelf Notable Indie award winner.

Kevin grew up in Wild Peach, Texas, where he was raised by his grandparents and given a healthy respect for story telling. He often found himself in trouble in school for writing stories instead of doing his actual assignments.

Kevin's love for history, archaeology, and science has been a tremendous source of material for his writing, feeding his fiction and giving him just the excuse he needs to read the next article, biography, or research paper.

Connect with Kevin:
kevintumlinson.com
kevin@tumlinson.net

facebook.com/jkevintumlinson

x.com/kevintumlinson

instagram.com/kevintumlinson

bookbub.com/authors/kevin-tumlinson

amazon.com/Kevin-Tumlinson/e/B007POXGEG

KEEP THE ADVENTURE GOING!

GET MORE THRILLS FROM AWARD-WINNING AND BESTSELLING AUTHOR, KEVIN TUMLINSON!

★★★★★ "Half way through I was waiting for Harrison Ford to leap out of the pages!"
—Deanne, Review for *The Coelho Medallion*

★★★★★ "Kevin has crashed onto the action-thriller scene

as only an action-thriller author can: with provocative plot lines, unforgettable characters, and enough adrenaline to keep you awake all night."
—Nick Thacker, author of *Mark for Blood*

★★★★★ "Move over Daniel Silva, James Patterson, and Dan Brown."
—Chip Polk, Review for *The Atlantis Riddle*

★★★★★ "Move Over Indiana Jones, there is a New Dr. in Town!"
—Cycletrash, Review for *The Coelho Medallion*

★★★★★ "[Kevin Tumlinson] is what every writer should be—entertaining and thought-provoking."
— Shana Tehan, Press Secretary, U.S. House of Representatives

★★★★★ "I discovered Kevin Tumlinson from The Creative Penn podcast and immediately got his novel, Evergreen. I read it in like 3 seconds. It's the most fast-paced story I've encountered."
—R.D. Holland, Independent Reviewer

★★★★★ "Comparison to Clive Cussler is a natural, though Tumlinson's 'Dan ' is more like Dan Brown's Robert Langdon than Dirk Pitt."
—Amazon Review for *The Coelho Medallion*

FIND YOUR NEXT FAVORITE BOOK AT
KevinTumlinson.com/books

www.ingramcontent.com/pod-product-compliance
Lightning Source LLC
Chambersburg PA
CBHW050506260626
47157CB00004B/1210